KENDALL RYAN

About the Book

Knox Bauer's life has unraveled to the point of no return. Fighting to fill the emptiness inside himself, he seeks solace in unfamiliar beds with unfamiliar women. As guardian to his three younger brothers, he can't seem to do anything right. But this can't go on...they look up to him in every way, and all he's done lately is prove how messed up he really is. Needing a change, he attends a local Sex Addicts Anonymous meeting, where he finds himself tempted by the wholesome yet alluring instructor, McKenna.-

Twenty-one-year-old McKenna is trying to make amends. After losing her parents in a horrific accident, she knows if she can just be good enough, maybe she can forgive herself for what happened. With her newly acquired degree in counseling, she begins leading a sex addicts group where she meets the troubled Knox, and her life takes on complications she never bargained for. She doesn't have time for a bad boy who only wants to take her to bed, even if her body disagrees. The fixer in her wants to help, but trusting Knox's true motivations might take more courage than she has.

When I Break is Book 1 in a new series.

Table of Contents

Chapter One

Pain exploded in my hand and I fell back onto the scuffed wooden floor. I stared down at the blood dripping from my shredded knuckles, and it took me a moment to place the shrill noise coming from behind me.

"Knox!" a girl screamed.

She knew my name, but I couldn't remember hers.

The girl's voice wasn't familiar. Probably because we hadn't done much talking when I brought her home last night. I wondered if the screams and moans she let out during sex would be more familiar to me. Probably not; I was pretty wasted when we'd gotten here.

Through blurry eyes, I looked at the girl for the first time, trying to remember where I'd picked her up. At the moment she was topless and wearing only a glittery pink thong. Images of her shaking her ass in that thong flooded my brain.

Tears welled in her eyes and she crept closer to me.

6

"Are you okay?"

The G-string she wore jogged my memory. Lap dance...dollar bills...shots of Cuervo burning a wicked path down my throat until my mind was just where I needed it. Oblivion.

"Knox, oh my God. What did you do?" She looked down, inspecting my hand more closely.

I closed my eyes for a moment, willing her to quiet down before she woke up my brothers. When I opened them again, I looked down and took stock of myself, naked and sitting sprawled on my bedroom floor. It wasn't one of my finer moments. I straightened my fingers, then hissed through clenched teeth as I inspected my injured hand in the dim light. *Shit.* I wasn't sure if it was broken, but it throbbed like a bitch.

"I'm fine," I bit out. My heart pounded in my chest and I was breathless, as if I'd just finished running a sprint. Blood smears painted the wall where I'd taken out my aggression, and a ragged hole gaped in the drywall. As I took deep breaths, trying to calm myself, I realized I'd been having a dream about what I would do to my father if I ever saw him again.

"Do you want me to get you something for the

7

pain?" the girl asked.

A distant memory flooded my brain, probably what brought on the nightmare in the first place. Images of my leg, broken and twisted when I'd fallen from a tree as a boy, suddenly came back to me. I remember putting on a brave face when my dad referred to pain pills as "bitch mints."

I shook my head. "No, I'm fine." I didn't need them then and I didn't need them now.

The girl sucked her lower lip into her mouth, her eyes welling with tears. There was nothing I hated more than seeing a girl cry.

"Come here." I reached my good hand toward her.

Her expression wary, she crawled over to where I sat on the floor. When I rose to my knees and stroked my lengthening dick, her eyes locked onto my movements, darting back and forth between my face, my bloodied hand, and my cock, trying to understand what I wanted.

"Come suck me off." Yeah, it was a dick move, but it was the only thing that would calm me down right now. It was either that or liquor, and I knew my cabinets would be empty. If I'd gone out earlier, it was most likely for alcohol, pussy, or both.

She frowned. "What about your hand?"

"Fuck my hand," I ground out. "I want your lips around my cock."

Wordlessly she obeyed, crawling the rest of the way toward me and leaning down to take me in her mouth. I fisted my bloodied hand in her hair, watching the curve of her back as she moved up and down over me, liking the feel of raw power and satisfaction it gave me.

Within minutes, I tapped her on the shoulder and she moved away as I finished with my hand, spurting into her open mouth. "Good girl." I petted her hair and she blinked up at me.

I rose and headed into the bathroom to clean myself off. "You can go now," I called out to her where she still sat on the floor, looking confused.

"But it's three in the morning."

"I don't care. Get the fuck out. You got what you came for." I tossed the bloodied towel to the bathroom floor and inspected my hand. The skin was torn at the knuckles, but nothing felt broken as I spread my fingers apart and rotated my wrist. I'd live.

9

"You don't have to be such an asshole," she yelled, gathering up her clothes and dressing hastily. "There's something wrong with you, you know that?"

Her hurt expression should have caused me to feel something. Remorse, regret, sympathy…something. But my battered body and fucked-up mind had stopped responding to normal human emotions years ago. I lived according to my baser instincts now. It was just easier that way.

"I know," I murmured. There was more wrong with me than she'd ever know.

The following morning I woke up late, my hand still throbbing. Crawling from bed, I twisted open a bottle of Jack that I'd found conveniently tucked under my pillow and took a healthy swig, then tucked it back under my pillow for safekeeping. I might be a mess, but I didn't want my younger brothers to pick up my nasty habits.

My cell phone vibrated from the rickety table by the door. The cell phone was new, as was my number, so I couldn't figure out who might be calling me. I glanced at the screen. *Fuck.* It was my therapist's office, reminding me of my appointment that afternoon. The last thing I wanted to do was go in and talk to some dickhead therapist about my feelings. But it was all part of my plea bargain. I had my choice: therapy or jail. Fucking DUI.

It just didn't seem fair. I'd tried to do all the right things since our father left—I worked hard all week, took care of my brothers, and paid the bills. But when I sought a little relief during my free time, I always found myself in a pile of shit.

But I couldn't think about that right now. If I did, I'd start drinking and either show up drunk to my first appointment, or not show up at all. Neither of which was a good option.

When I arrived at the office, the soft music and scattered couches in the waiting room already had me on edge. I didn't want to be here. Knowing I didn't have much of a choice, I approached the receptionist at the desk, a meek little thing with brown hair pulled into a ponytail. Big green eyes looked straight up at me.

"Knox Bauer. I have an appointment at three o'clock."

"Hi. Could you sign in right here?" She tapped the clipboard on the counter.

11

I signed my name and took a seat. A moment later, she scurried around the desk and handed me a clipboard of forms. "Since it's your first time here, can you fill these out?"

I took the papers without a word and watched as she sauntered away, her ass bouncing in the most delectable way in her knee-length skirt. I hadn't seen a girl dress like that in a while. All prim and proper. She was sending off schoolmarm vibes, which my dick told me I found refreshing. I guess I'd been hanging out with strippers too much, not that I was about to reevaluate the company I kept. No, they served a distinct and necessary purpose in my life.

I shook the thoughts away and focused on the forms. Once I turned them in, I was escorted by the receptionist with the nice ass into the therapist's office.

"Knox?" An aging woman with gray hair greeted me, rising from behind her desk.

"Yup." I strode into the office, hearing the soft click as the receptionist closed the door behind me.

"I'm Dr. Claudia Lowe. Have a seat."

I obeyed, lowering myself to the stiff leather arm

chair in front of her desk. No sense in pissing off the good doctor straight away. I'd play nice. For now.

We sat facing each other, her appraising me coolly over the rim of lowered spectacles. "I trust you know why you're here?"

I nodded.

"I see a lot of anger management cases. Most are men with a history of fighting or domestic abuse. Your case is something altogether different. I trust you know that too."

I nodded again. Oh yeah, I'd gotten myself in a pile of shit, all right. After a night out drinking last summer, I'd stupidly driven home and gotten a DUI. Because it was my first offense and my court-appointed attorney played the sympathy card, explaining to the judge I was caring for my minor siblings, I was let off easy with fines and community service. Then after I'd brilliantly smarted off to the judge, he'd tacked on an order to see a counselor for anger management.

The first shrink I'd seen had dug into my brain, and concluded pretty quickly that my issues weren't related to anger. After a battery of questions about my past and how I dealt with the stress in my life, she became convinced I had an issue with sex and referred me to Dr. Lowe. I

13

didn't think fucking was a crime, but apparently the counselor had felt differently. She'd written up some shit about stress being relived in sexual ways, and that I lacked the ability to form and maintain healthy relationships with the opposite sex. Bullshit. I was just horny.

I glanced up at Dr. Lowe, who was reading from a page in front of her. "When you were fifteen, you got kicked out of school for engaging in indecent acts with a female student."

"I don't see how my high school flings have anything to do with this."

She smiled tightly. "Nothing is off-limits in our sessions together, Mr. Bauer. Just because it's not officially on your record doesn't mean we're not going to discuss it."

I ground my teeth, and she pushed on. "When you were seventeen, you were sent to a boot-camp-style high school during your senior year. Three months later, you were arrested for public drunkenness and lewd behavior."

I sighed. "My buddies and I had our first night out in months. I got drunk and I took a girl out in the back alleyway. I wasn't hurting anyone, just blowing off some steam. And trust me, she was willing." The woman

14

probably wouldn't care that it was around that same time that my father had left us, so I didn't mention it.

She leaned forward, removing her glasses and resting her elbows on the desk. "I know you feel these instances can be explained away, but you have a history of using sex to cope. And after gaining legal custody of your brothers—"

"I'm not discussing that with you."

She nodded. "Not yet."

Motherfu— I cursed under my breath. No one needed to know our family business. I took good care of the boys. They weren't part of this. I intentionally kept this side of myself from them.

"I'm recommending something a bit unconventional for your treatment. I would like you to join a local Sex Addicts Anonymous support group."

Sex addict? My jaw tightened. I wasn't a fucking sex addict. I liked pussy. There was a difference. A big fucking difference.

"Your sexual past has been noted, and according to your own admissions, you've had more partners than you can recall and you use sex as an escape."

She glared at me, waiting for me to disagree. I bit my cheek and stayed quiet. It was true I thought about sex a lot. All the time, actually. But I thought most guys did. Though, if I were being honest, I knew I was worse than my buddies. When I was younger they'd nicknamed me Worm, because of how many girl's panties I'd wormed my way into over the years. I wasn't an addict, though; I was an opportunist. I'd never turn down a willing female.

"This field of study is just emerging but most researchers agree, the definition of a sex addict is someone whose deviant sexual behavior interferes with daily life— their relationships, job, et cetera."

Well, shit. I wouldn't fight her on this. I was radioactive. An asshole. A user of women, but shit, they'd all been willing. Maybe she was right, though. I hated the tears and drama that came with my less-than-stellar behavior toward the opposite sex. And the last thing I wanted was my behavior to rub off on my brothers. I wanted better for them.

Dr. Lowe scribbled something on a piece of paper. "Here's the group you'll be attending. First meeting is tomorrow morning and they meet weekly. I'll receive reports on your progress and what you're learning about

16

yourself during these group sessions. If you progress well, I'll be able to note that in my letter to the judge. The choice is yours."

She shoved the paper at me.

"Okay." I kept my voice neutral as I picked up the paper, but inside? Inside, I was fighting the urge to curse and crumple it into a ball.

This was bullshit.

Chapter Two

I closed my eyes and said a silent prayer. I needed to stop my hands from shaking. This was going to be fine. I could do this. My pep talk did little good, though; I knew how pathetic I was. A sexual addiction counselor and technically still a virgin.

It wasn't from lack of effort on my part. I'd made up my mind my sophomore year of college and decided to have sex with my boyfriend at the time, Jason. He'd been thrilled, of course; I'd made him wait six long months with only heavy make-out sessions to sustain him. He'd been weird about sex—often leaving me to initiate things and tell him when I was ready for more—which only made me feel undesired and insecure. I didn't know what I was doing. I wanted him to take the lead, but never had the courage to tell him.

When I finally told him I was ready, we were in the backseat of his Toyota Prius, since we were both too embarrassed to tell our dorm roommates that we needed some privacy. He'd done it before but seemed almost more timid than me, repositioning us over and over in the tiny car, and then losing his erection when he'd finally slipped on the condom. I felt like a failure. Like it was somehow my fault, and it wasn't an experience I wanted to repeat. So I hadn't.

The only part of being a virgin that bugged me was that if anyone here knew, I was sure I'd be a laughingstock.

But I thrust my shoulders back, ready, or at least ready to fake it for my first solo group session without my mentor, Belinda. I could do this. I'd be fine. It was a different group than the one I'd trained with. Belinda had recommended that, which I thought was good advice.

I'd gotten to know the roughly dozen or so regulars who attended her Tuesday night meeting. I'd become familiar with their stories—like Pamela, the sweet Italian girl who was always looking for love, trying to make up for her father's rejection. Or Ted, the middle-aged businessman who'd become addicted to Internet porn during the economic downturn when he was laid off and home alone every day. Bored and horny.

Today I'd have a whole new group to get to know, the Saturday morning group. As scary as it was, this was a

19

fresh start. This group wouldn't see me as just the trainee. I was the group leader. I'd studied for this, gone to school for this. But that didn't mean my stomach wasn't flipping violently when the doors opened and the first person entered the room.

An older man with hair graying at his temples.

I smiled warmly, then averted my eyes and went back to organizing the papers on my desk. I didn't want him to feel watched or uncomfortable in my presence. There was a fine line between being friendly and open, and giving people their space. I certainly never wanted anyone here to feel judged.

The room began to fill, people mingling near the coffeepot, making small talk about the weather or local sports teams—discussing anything but the reason we were all gathered here. Most were middle-aged men, not surprising there, it was the same with my last group. But a few younger people and women made it a little more diverse.

When everyone had taken a seat in one of the chairs arranged into a semicircle in the center of the room, I was just about to take the spot at the front when a guy about my age, looking tense and unsure, opened the door and

20

just stood there.

He was tall and extremely fit with wide shoulders and a toned chest, hinted at by the way his T-shirt clung to him. His hair was cropped close, just long enough to be messy in the front. But his deep, expressive eyes were his most stunning feature—a mix of dark hazel and warm brown framed in thick lashes and bright with intelligence.

For a split second I struggled to pull my gaze away from his. I'd appreciated attractive men before, but this man possessed a magnetism that made it impossible for me to look away. My heart thundered in my chest while I stared, mouth open, watching him.

His hand curled around the doorknob, but he made no move to enter. He was obviously new here. And by the looks of it, about to flee.

"Are you here for SAA?" Our abbreviation for sex addicts anonymous. "Come on in, we're just about to start." I found my voice and motioned him forward.

He swallowed hard, his throat contracting as emotions flashed across his face. Then his expression hardened and he entered the room, letting the heavy door fall closed behind him with a thud.

Mister Tall, Dark, and Devastatingly Handsome took the last open seat, the one directly across from me, and raked his gaze over my skin. A hot shudder passed through me and I fought to control my nerves. Something about having to address the group with his dark eyes on me made me incredibly nervous.

I cleared my throat and began. "Welcome. This is a support group for people with sexual addiction. I've been working with another group, so I wanted to take a moment to introduce myself, and then I'll ask you to do the same."

I folded my hands in my lap and began, my eyes looking anywhere but at the guy across from me. He was too distracting.

"My name is McKenna, and I've been leading another SAA group for six months. I have a bachelor's degree in counseling and I also work at a center for troubled teens. In my free time, I like volunteering and watching scary movies."

I smiled warmly. "I'd like everyone to introduce themselves, tell us a bit about yourself, and if you're comfortable, why you're here." I turned to the gentlemen to my left and nodded, thankful that I'd gotten through that with my voice steady and composed.

One by one each person introduced themselves, most giving a brief snippet about why they were here. Their revelations were vague and general, saying only things like *I need help to get my life back on track.* That was to be expected; we'd work our way up to the more personal confessions as time went on.

When everyone else had spoken, my eyes went to the beautiful stranger seated across from me. He cleared his throat and fidgeted in the chair, eliciting a loud squeal as the metal legs shifted against the tile floor. Something in his posture told me he had no plans to share anything about himself. Active group participation was a strong indicator of belief in the program, and one's ability to successfully overcome their addiction.

I frowned, realizing he might be here for the wrong reasons. A college kid on a dare from his friends, or a way to pick up easy women. I wasn't sure, so I fixed him with a stare.

"To be part of this meeting you must admit you have a problem, and that your life has become unmanageable and you need help. You must commit to attending the meetings and to sharing with the group."

The newcomer rolled his eyes. "My name's Knox Bauer. I'm a Virgo and I like long walks on the beach."

I released the little breath I'd been holding. It seemed we might have a problem, one I'd have to address after group. I'd seen Belinda do the same thing before, to make sure everyone was here for the right reason.

I pushed on, ignoring his blatant disregard for the group—for now. Finally the clock on the wall indicated our hour was up, which was good because I couldn't take another second of his eyes watching my every move. I felt distracted and itchy, and fought the urge to run—to flee this room and Knox's heated stare. But I told myself to calm down. I could handle this. Too bad my training in no way prepared me for a super-hot alpha male invading my space.

After putting on a sincere smile, I wrapped up the meeting with, "Thank you, everyone. I'll see you next Saturday and in the meantime, stay strong. And remember you can call me or your sponsor at any time."

I breathed a sigh of relief. My first solo group had gone pretty well. All except for the newcomer, Knox, who seemed reluctant to take part in the group. It was time to address the issue head-on.

My eyes went to Knox, who was already rising from his chair. "Knox, can you stay behind a minute?"

He hesitated briefly, obviously thinking it over, and then lowered himself back to the metal folding chair.

The room was too small, too warm, and I crossed the room to adjust the ancient thermostat on the far wall. I didn't even know if it worked, but the chance to get out of Knox's line of vision for just a moment was a welcome reprieve. I pushed the switch to the coolest setting and sucked in a few deep breaths.

I returned to stand in front of Knox. His smile was playful as his eyes wandered the length of my body. His look was so sexual, so erotic, that my stomach twirled into a series of intricate knots and my knees trembled where I stood.

Chapter Three

The overpowering scent of citrus floor polish was giving me a headache. I wanted nothing more than to escape, but I nodded in response to McKenna's request, lowering myself back down to the seat. Evidently I was about to catch shit for not sharing my feelings in this damn circle jerk of a meeting.

The people around me rose and filed from the room. I didn't know what I expected sex addicts to look like, but it certainly wasn't this. They looked like regular people, for the most part. Guys like me.

McKenna crossed the room to fiddle with the thermostat on the wall, seeming to buy her time, and then approached me once again.

I couldn't resist letting my gaze slip down over her curves. Her confidence wavered as her eyes dropped from mine to the floor between her feet. There was something about me that threw her off her game. As confident as she'd been during the meeting, her self-assurance wavered as she stood before me.

Petite, but with nice curves, she was stunning. She had long glossy hair hanging down her back and delicate features—a small nose, wide eyes, and high cheekbones. I'd be blind not to notice how attractive she was. Her eyes darted everywhere but on me, letting me take my fill uninterrupted. Wasn't there some saying about never trust a skinny chef? Well, never trust a beautiful sex-addiction counselor either. Or perhaps it was that I didn't trust myself around her.

As I studied her, I realized she wasn't like the girls I hung around. She was beautiful. Educated. Intelligent. Submissive. It was that last part that got my blood pumping south. Introducing her to the business end of my dick became priority number one, but then my lurid thoughts screeched to a halt. I cursed under my breath. That wasn't in the cards. I needed to remember why I was here.

McKenna sat down in the chair beside me, her hands moving restlessly in her lap. "I think we got off on the wrong foot," she murmured. "I'm here to help. That's all." She held up her hands, palms out in a placating gesture, and her eyes met mine.

Her hands were small and looked soft. It had been a while since I'd been around a girl as innocent and pure as she seemed to be. I nodded, acknowledging her statement, then cleared my throat and asked, "Did you need something?" She had asked me to stay behind, after all.

She took a deep breath, inhaling slowly, as if to steady herself. "Success in this program hinges on one's ability to admit they have a problem with sexual activity, and that they need help."

Although I could surely use her help with some sexual activity, I had a feeling that wasn't what she meant.

"I'm here at the request of my counselor." My voice was bland, indicating my lack of passion regarding her little meetings.

She looked down at the floor to the space between our feet once again, momentarily falling silent before raising her gaze to mine once again. "What do you do for fun, Mr. Bauer? To blow off steam."

Mr. Bauer. I liked the sound of that falling from her pink lips way too much. My gaze zeroed in on her mouth, and McKenna bit down on her lower lip.

I stuffed my hands into my pockets, forcing my eyes

away. "What do you want to know?"

"Your hobbies."

My hobbies? Drinking, getting arrested, fucking pretty little things like her. Since the truth would shock her, I just shrugged. "Nothing that concerns you, angel."

"You're awfully...dominant, aren't you?" Her words were direct, but her gaze remained glued to the floor, as if she was unable to be so bold while holding my eyes. It set off something inside me.

I didn't like the label. *Dominant.* I'd read a little bit about it online, and I'd be lying if some of the shit I read didn't ring true. I liked to take control in the bedroom. Give orders. Be pleased by a girl eager to submit, or give pleasure to someone so willing to receive it. I liked the control it gave. The heady feeling of power. Especially because there was so much in my life I couldn't control. And something about McKenna's gentle nature told me if I could get past her walls, she would submit to me beautifully.

I was even sicker and more fucked up than she knew. I'd own her. But as fun as it might be, I wouldn't let myself break her. She was my sexual addiction counselor. She was off-limits. And it wasn't like I had an actual problem. I liked sex. I was a red-blooded American male, but I could control myself.

"Your reaction is very common, Mr. Bauer," she went on. "With all due respect, it sounds like you may be in denial, especially if you continue to engage in destructive sexual activities."

I let out a snort. "You think you're going to cure me of wanting sex, angel? Not a chance." The nickname slid from my lips with ease. She was a sweet, blue-eyed, petite little thing. Soft and innocent looking too. An angel amongst devils.

"We don't preach celibacy. That's not what I'm asking of you." Her voice wavered ever so slightly.

"Damn good thing too." No way in fuck was I taking a vow of abstinence. I felt itchy and uncomfortable just thinking about it, like a caged animal ready to rebel. Why was I letting her get under my skin? *Shit.*

"We operate under the same approach as many twelve-step programs. We don't expect abstinence, but my goal is to help you engage in healthy sexual activity. To work with you to stay away from people or images that might trigger compulsive sexual behavior."

This was insane. I wasn't some sicko, some sexual deviant. I just really, really liked women. I shouldn't have even come here today. I should have told that counselor to fuck off instead of agreeing to this bullshit interrogation. My heartbeat pounded in my ears, and I crossed my arms over my chest to hide my clenched fists.

"Our group members often have unresolved emotional issues, things from their pasts that bring on PTSD, anxiety, depression. Eighty percent of sex addicts were abused as children…" McKenna prattled on like she was reading from a textbook.

My past had nothing to do with my liking sex. The only thing that kept me in my seat was watching McKenna's pretty blue eyes looking so solemnly at mine. She held me captive, even if I didn't want to listen to what she had to say.

McKenna licked her lips slightly, which made my dick twitch, and said, "Only once you deal with your sexual dysfunction can you form true, loving relationships, and break the cycle."

No thanks. Been there, done that. And I had the battle scars to prove it. I shifted in my seat, becoming more agitated by the second.

She leaned forward, her expression sincere. "You can't do this alone, in private by yourself, Knox. I'm here to help."

"Sex feels good, McKenna," I spat out. "You should try it. It releases endorphins."

"So does jogging."

I couldn't help the throaty chuckle that tore from my chest. Jogging as a replacement for sex? This girl was crazy.

"I have to go." I shot to my feet, needing out of this room where her sweet scent was invading my senses and making my head spin.

McKenna opened her mouth to argue, but closed it once I stood.

We were done. At least for now.

Chapter Four

That night while lying in bed, I couldn't stop myself from thinking about him. Knox Bauer. Even his name rolling off my lips sent my pulse racing.

I pulled the freshly washed sheets up to my chin and closed my eyes, trying to clear the thoughts swirling inside my head. I knew all too well that morning would come too soon, and I needed my rest. Tomorrow I was on call at the teen shelter; I'd volunteered to be put into their regular rotation of staffers. It was a big commitment but it kept me busy, which I preferred.

Even as I lay warm and cozy in my big empty bed, my thoughts flitted back to the gorgeous stranger who had given off such a mysterious and commanding vibe. I thought about how wounded he was. How high he'd built up his walls. I plotted various ways to reach him, to get through to him and help. Of course, I knew from years of schooling that successful treatment hinged on the patient actually wanting to get better. And something told me

Knox didn't. He seemed comfortable with himself and his sexuality.

I'd be lying to myself if I said I didn't notice him physically. My undersexed body was highly aware of him. His masculine scent—crisp cotton and spicy aftershave with hints of sandalwood and leather. The five o'clock shadow that I was sure would rasp against my skin if he kissed me, and the deep timbre of his rough voice. It was a lethal combination that did something to me. The man was trouble, a sexy-as-hell troublemaker, but still. It bothered me that I couldn't turn off my thoughts.

Most of the night I tossed and turned, unable to forget the way Knox's messy disheveled hair made him look both sexy and dangerous at the same time. The way his dark eyes pierced mine, forcing the air from my lungs.

It was my job to help him, not lust after him. I'd need to follow the advice from my own lessons when he was near—counting backward from ten, taking deep, calming breaths. That is, if he ever showed up again. He seemed adamant that he didn't belong there, and I wouldn't be at all surprised if he dropped out altogether.

What seemed like only minutes later, my alarm went off, startling me awake.

While the water heated for my shower, I dragged myself to the sink to brush my teeth. I was nothing if not efficient. After stepping into the steaming water, I cranked it as hot as I could stand. The heat enveloped me and soothed my aching shoulders. I was exhausted and struggled to remember why, what I did yesterday to wear me out.

A vision of Knox's chiseled features invaded my mind. Oh yeah. I suppressed a shiver racing down my spine and through my belly and pressed a hand against the wet tile wall, supporting the sudden jolt at the memory of him. I'd never had that weak-in-the-knees, butterflies-in-the-stomach feeling before. I'd thought it was all a myth. But it seemed Knox was the one man who had broken through my defenses.

Too bad he was off-limits and I could do nothing about it.

Chapter Five

How your life could change so drastically over the course of a few years was crazy. I could have never imagined that at age eighteen I'd be financially and legally responsible for my three younger brothers.

But when my dad left four years ago, there was no way in fuck I was letting us get split up and sent into the foster care system. We'd been through enough. After losing Mom, and then Dad turning out to be a selfish prick, we had to stick together. Tucker had only been four, and Luke and Jaxon just thirteen and fourteen at the time. I'd graduated early from high school and began working full-time to meet our rent, utilities, and grocery bills. That first year was a blur. We had peanut butter sandwiches for dinner when money was tight, and endured the heat and electricity getting turned off more than once that first year. Things had gotten a little better since then, but it was still hard.

I knew I used girls to forget pain, to mask my

emotions, and of course to feel pleasure. That had begun when I was still in high school. I also knew I had no plans to change it. Just because I was in some ridiculous sex addicts group didn't mean I need to go all holier-than-thou and reform myself. Fuck that. My lifestyle was the only thing keeping me sane at the moment. The only thing keeping me out of jail, most likely. I might tone it down for my brothers' sake, but I wasn't about to change who I was.

All week long I'd worked, hit the gym, hung out at home with my brothers, and looked forward to seeing McKenna again. I knew it was stupid. She was my sexual addiction counselor, for fuck's sake. I was delusional thinking there could be something between us, yet I knew she felt the raw magnetism just like I had. I'd seen it in her eyes. Her curiosity had been unmistakable. The soft inhalation of breath, her fluttering pulse, calling me "Mr. Bauer." Shit, I had liked that way too much.

After a late-afternoon jog where I'd let the smoggy heat of Chicago drench me in sweat, I showered, dressed, then made the boys a snack just as they were arriving home from school. It was one of the rules I enforced— straight home after school, homework and family dinner, and then friends or other social activities. The front door

37

burst open and a pile of backpacks, shoes, and lunch boxes hit the foyer floor. Jaxon disappeared up the stairs as Luke and Tucker tore into the kitchen, stealing crackers and slices of cheese from the counter where I'd placed them.

"What's wrong with Jaxon?" I asked.

"He has to poop." Tucker giggled.

I smiled. Sometimes I felt pretty damn lucky to live with only guys. We said what was on our minds, took care of business, and didn't overanalyze things. It was a pretty sweet deal.

Minutes later Jaxon appeared, looking sullen. Even though he was the oldest, I worried about him more than the other two. He was in his final year of high school with no clue what he wanted to do afterward.

I leaned against the counter, watching them munch on crackers and listening to stories about school. Tucker wandered away after having his fill, and I brushed the crumbs he left behind into the sink.

"Is everything okay, Knox? I heard screaming coming from your room the other night," Jaxon asked.

Jaxon was the most like me, which meant he was also the most suspicious, especially after my arrest for a DUI. I could understand their concern. I was the only guardian they had—I couldn't go off the deep end like that again. And I refused to let them down; that would make me no better than our father.

Embarrassed, I scrubbed a hand over my face. "No. But it will be. In fact, I wanted to tell you that I've begun attending a class Saturday mornings to put my life back on track."

"Is it the anger management class the judge wanted you to take?" Luke, my seventeen-year-old brother asked. His watchful eyes waited for my response.

With Tucker in his bedroom, playing superheroes by the sound of it, I figured Luke and Jaxon were old enough to know the truth. I didn't shield them from much. To me, that was no different than lying. My father was a liar, and I didn't care to walk in his footsteps in any regard.

I took a deep breath. The first step was admitting you had a problem, right? "The counselor actually wants me to attend a group for people with sexual addiction. She thought my history with girls was…too much."

"And that's a bad thing?" Jaxon asked, a hint of a smile playing at the edges of his mouth. He was way too much like me. And the several high school girls I'd found crying at our doorstep proved his track record was already eerily similar to mine.

I needed to find a way to get through to him. But I guess getting my own life on track was the first step.

Chapter Six

Friday nights were the hardest for me. I had thought moving to Chicago would be my chance to break free, the beginning of a grand and exciting adventure. But so far, my life here had been anything but.

I worked, I volunteered, and I went home to the quiet little apartment I shared with Brian. Then I'd change into my pajamas and heat up a can of soup for dinner each night while watching sitcom reruns in my bedroom. When I thought about how different my life was from that of other girls my age, it didn't even seem like we were on the same planet. Going out dancing, dating, going to clubs…all of it felt so far out of reach for me.

I had always thought there would be time for fun later, like I was in a holding pattern waiting for my real life to start. As if all this was temporary. Someday I'd meet someone, forgive myself, and all the stress and guilt I carried around with me would suddenly vanish. I knew it didn't work that way, but it was a pretty thought.

While I was growing up, school and grades had always been more important than boys and parties. Plus, I was what you'd call a late bloomer. Braces and glasses hampered my social life throughout high school, as well as a layer of acne, thanks to the greasy pizza place I worked at after school. After the accident, a social life and dates to dances were the last things I cared about. It had all been about surviving.

Needing some independence from the little Indiana town where I grew up, I'd jumped at the chance when I was offered a job in Chicago to counsel troubled teens. Besides, there was nothing for me back in Indiana anymore.

After my parents passed away tragically in a car accident my senior year of high school, I'd stayed with my friend Brian and his parents so I could finish the school year. Each day I kept my head down and did what was expected of me, then each night I cried myself to sleep. After graduation, I attended a local community college and continued living with Brian's parents, even when he moved two hours away to go to Indiana University.

I had moved to Chicago to be free, to start over. But of course that wasn't possible. My past followed me, just like it always would. Brian decided to relocate along with me, saying he would never let me fend for myself alone in the big city. Even though that had been exactly what I'd wanted. A fresh start where no one knew me as the sad little orphaned girl.

Did I want to live with Brian? No, but affording my own place in Chicago was out of the question. We'd found a two-bedroom, two-bathroom apartment, so at least we each had our own space. There was also a large kitchen and living room, and a small den where we put a breakfast table and my bookshelves. Brian had painted it a sunny yellow for me, even though we'd have to change it back to white when we moved out, per the landlord's orders.

I should have been grateful, but his presence was a constant reminder of what had happened. Of who I'd become. I was living as a shell of my former self without any idea how to break free.

I pushed all that from my mind when I heard Brian knock at my bedroom door. Fixing on a pleasant smile, I pulled it open and stepped out into the hall. "Hi."

"Hey, you." He pulled me warmly into a hug, and I didn't fight it. It was the only physical affection I got. And Brian was comfortable, like your favorite tennis shoes.

"You ready?" he asked.

"Yep." I grabbed my purse from the counter and looped it around my body.

Brian had bought a Groupon for a painting class tonight, and invited me along. He knew I wasn't a go-out-and-party type, and his attempts at taking me out to dinner had failed too. It felt too much like a date, so we stuck to simple activities like this. Safe. Platonic. The story of my life.

When I thought about my meeting in the morning, the prospect of seeing Knox again sent a little thrill through me, making my belly dance with nerves. All week while I worked with the teen girls at the center, I'd felt like a hypocrite. I counseled them about not making their whole life about a guy, yet here I was, all my waking thoughts consumed by the mystery that was Knox Bauer.

"You okay?" Brian squinted at me.

"Fine." I squirmed, forcing the thoughts of Knox's raw masculinity from my brain. "Let's go get our painting on."

Chapter Seven

After a trying week with my brothers, the last thing I wanted to do was go to my Sex Addicts Anonymous meeting—but the promise of seeing McKenna there forced my hand. I wanted to watch the way her eyes gravitated toward mine, and the soft flush of pink that warmed her cheeks when she spoke. She was a curiosity. A fun plaything to entertain me since I had to sit through the torture of being there.

I stepped into a pair of jeans and shoved my feet into my worn boots before making my way downstairs. Tucker sped past me, tearing through the kitchen with a bowl of cereal in hand, sloshing milk on the wooden floor right at my feet. He beelined it for the TV to watch his Saturday morning cartoons. It was the only time I let him eat in front of the television, so instead of scolding him for the spilled milk, I dropped a kitchen rag to the floor and began mopping it up with my foot. The TV switched on and a roar of canned laughter came from the other room as I flung the milk-soaked cloth into the sink.

Our house wasn't clean. It wasn't organized. But we tried to keep it somewhat tidy. We each took turns washing the dishes and doing the laundry. The floors weren't mopped and the bathroom was often neglected, but we managed. We had clean dishes to eat from and fresh clothes to wear. It was all we needed.

During the week while the boys were at school, I managed a hardware store, and at night I occasionally picked up bartending shifts for the extra money. It provided enough to pay the bills, but bigger things weighed on me—paying for college, buying cell phones, and cars for the guys. I had no idea how any of that would be possible.

I tried to push those thoughts from my mind as I drove to my sex addicts meeting. I would deal with one problem at a time. It was all I could do.

When I arrived, the chairs were already filling up in a semicircle around McKenna. I grabbed a paper cup of weak coffee and sat down just as she was getting started. Her eyes flashed to mine and a tiny smile lifted her mouth. She hadn't thought I would show up, and her relief was visible. I couldn't help but give her my best panty-dropping grin and watched as her chest and neck flushed pink.

McKenna's eyes dropped down to the notes on her lap and she took a moment to steady herself before beginning. "Sex addicts are very me-centric. Your addiction isn't meant to serve anyone else. It's a selfish pursuit. You get what you want, when you want it. And that's why it can be so difficult to break. You're not used to having to delay gratification. Today I want you to think about how you first became dependent on sex."

She paused for a moment, her gaze drifting around the faces in the group. I couldn't help but notice she deliberately avoided looking my way. Apparently I rattled her and she needed her composure to continue the meeting.

How did I become dependent on sex? I wasn't sure I could pinpoint when it happened, but sure, I used sex to numb my pain and manage stress. Listening to McKenna, I was starting to believe that maybe it wasn't totally normal.

"Over time, people develop a tolerance for sex. They need more and more of it to feel okay, and they experience withdrawal if they can't have it. Eventually, it can destroy your relationships—your marriage, your job. I know we've previously talked about being fired for looking at Internet porn at work, or marriages ending when a spouse discovered an affair. Your risky behaviors put you in danger for contracting a life-threatening STD. Or put you in debt, paying for strip clubs and prostitutes. None of these things lead to good outcomes. Can anyone share some of the techniques they've developed to work through their cravings?"

Shit. She actually wanted people to share how they avoided sex? It would be more useful to share techniques on how I seduced girls from nightclubs, coffee shops, the grocery store, or how to fuck standing up in a tiny bathroom stall. Doggie style. It was really the only option.

A timid girl directly across from me cleared her throat. "I count backward from ten and practice deep, calming breaths."

"That's great, Mia. Anyone else?" McKenna asked, looking straight at me this time.

I wasn't saying shit.

Watching McKenna was hypnotic. After our last little exchange, I hadn't been able to get her out of my mind, and seeing her in person, I completely got why. She was soft and pretty. Her voice was light, clear, and appealing.

Listening to her and watching the way her mouth moved around her words penetrated my walls, reached deep inside me and went straight to my dick. I had no idea why she'd have such a profound effect on me—unless it was a simple case of wanting what I couldn't have. I wanted to unbutton her white shirt, push it open, and rub my fingertips over her nipples until she sucked in a deep, shuddery breath. I wanted to see what kind of panties she wore and break down her walls, like she was doing to me.

Holy shit. Maybe I did have a problem. I was sitting in a sex addicts meeting with a hard-on. I was pretty sure that couldn't be filed under N for normal.

But shit, I wasn't like these people. Was I? The fucking jackass next to me was dressed in sweatpants with a hole in the crotch, and he'd just spent twenty minutes confessing about how he'd jacked off in the car to porn downloaded on his phone before coming into the meeting. I scooted my chair farther away from him and caught a glare from McKenna.

McKenna continued providing prompts in the conversation and several more people opened up. By the time the hour was up, I knew far more about the people sitting around me than I wanted to.

A few group members still lingered as I approached McKenna at the front of the room, where she was leaning against a table near the window. I wondered if she was going to chastise me for not talking again.

"Still afraid to open up?" she asked, peeking up at me through thick lashes.

I wasn't afraid, but I knew what she was trying to do. She wanted to goad me into talking.

"I don't like this sharing bullshit in the group. I'm not saying I won't talk to you—I will. Me and you. Someplace else. Private."

She narrowed her eyes, searching mine. "You think you're the first guy in this group to hit on me? Not by a long shot. I'm here to do a job, Knox. That's all."

I chuckled. She thought I was asking her out? That was ridiculous; I didn't take girls out.

"Don't judge me. You and your charmed life you lead—you don't know anything about my life, sweetheart. And P.S. I'm here because I choose to be here."

"McKenna?" a tall, lanky guy called out from the doorway. "Everything okay?"

I looked his way, noting that I hadn't seen him in the

group before, yet he seemed pretty familiar with McKenna.

"Brian? What are you doing here?"

"I thought you might like a ride home. Is everything all right?" His gaze moved between me and her, his expression radiating concern.

McKenna swallowed and glanced at me before answering. "It's fine." She nodded. "And I told you, I'm fine taking the bus."

"Are you sure?"

McKenna fixed her friend with an icy stare, sending her message loud and clear without words.

"Okay," he said, stuffing his hands in his pockets. "I guess I'll see you at home later."

"Bye, Brian."

Brian nodded and left reluctantly, leaving McKenna and me alone once again.

When she turned to face me again, I could see judgment written all over her pretty face. I was beneath her. She'd labeled me and stuck me in some damn box. Hell, I knew I wasn't good enough for a girl like her, but I hadn't expected for her to actually call me out on it.

I fixed a sneer on my face. "Better go get home safe and sound, away from all us fuck-ups, McKenna." Then I turned for the door and strode away.

Chapter Eight

I could not have handled that worse. I hated the idea that I'd offended Knox; that was never my intention. Maybe he'd been serious about opening up one-on-one with me—perhaps it hadn't been a pick-up line at all. And I'd overreacted. Horribly. A sour pit sank low in my stomach and settled there.

I noticed a small leather-bound notebook resting against the desktop where Knox had been leaning. Crossing the room to retrieve the book, I wondered if there was a way to find him, to apologize and return his journal. I should have just waited to return it to him next Saturday, assuming he came back, but I knew that wasn't what I wanted.

This group was supposed to be anonymous, but Knox gave his last name at the first meeting—Bauer. And his first name wasn't all that common, so perhaps I'd have some luck finding him. I pulled out my smartphone and typed his name into Google: Kɴᴏx Bᴀᴜᴇʀ + Cʜɪᴄᴀɢᴏ, and was rewarded with an address. A home in the South Loop, not too far from where I lived.

Since I hadn't yet gotten around to buying a car, I took the city bus to a stop that would let me off two blocks from his neighborhood. Along the way, my mind drifted to Brian and the overprotective nature he'd been exhibiting lately. I knew I needed to have a talk with him soon.

After moving to Chicago, Brian had interviewed at several accounting firms in the city and quickly got multiple offers. He insisted that he wouldn't have me living by myself in a strange city, and changed his entire career plan for me. Living here alone was part of the appeal, but of course I hadn't argued. I had someone to hang out with Friday nights or go to the Laundromat with on Sundays. It was nice. And he was someone steady I could rely on. I couldn't really complain; he looked after me and I wasn't naive enough to think that a young girl alone in the city didn't need a friend.

Of course there was a chance he might read things wrong between us if we lived together. Sometimes the way he looked at me for too long made me wonder if he and I were on the same page about our friends-only relationship status. But he'd insisted, and I hadn't refused, even though I knew I'd never reciprocate any deeper feelings he might have. Maybe he was too safe a choice—he wasn't broken—there was nothing for me to fix, so he held no appeal. But either way, I just wasn't attracted to him that way.

My thoughts drifted as I stared out the window of the bus. Cars whizzed past and tall buildings loomed in the distance. There was a whole bustling world out there that I wasn't a part of. My life had become something almost unrecognizable. I knew how I'd gotten this way: one tiny step at a time. A few months after I lost my parents, I began volunteering. The grief counselor I saw at school thought it might help, and she was right. Caring for others got my mind off my grief and reminded me that not everyone led a charmed life. I spent time at the soup kitchen, the homeless shelter, a center for special needs kids. It became somewhat of an obsession. It was my escape from the harsh reality my life had become.

My parents' deaths had been my fault. Not literally, of course; I wasn't foolish enough to believe that. But in a small way, I was responsible, and that was all that mattered. There was no un-doing what I'd done. They'd died in a terrible car accident at the hands of a drunk driver on their way to church one Sunday. I still remembered every vivid detail about that morning.

I'd wanted to sleep in, as I often wanted to do on Sundays. It became a sticking point for me and my mom. We'd fight every weekend because I didn't care about going to church. I was too old for Sunday school and didn't see the importance of going. We'd argued that morning, and I'd screamed at them from my room and slammed the door in my mother's face. They'd left late because of me, much later than usual, and when they drove through the intersection of Main Street and Fourth, the drunk driver was there, running the red light just in time to slam into the passenger side door, killing my mom instantly and banging up my dad pretty badly. He was airlifted to a nearby hospital and died from bleeding inside his brain two days later.

If I'd just been selfless enough that Sunday morning and put my own needs aside, I would have gone with my parents. They wouldn't have left late, and they'd still be alive. But they weren't, which was why I worked so hard to make amends for their deaths. It couldn't be all for nothing.

Glancing at nearby passengers, I brushed at my

cheeks, wiping away a few tears that had sneaked past my defenses. I took a few deep breaths, willing myself to think about something different, and clasped the journal tightly on my lap.

The journal. I hadn't intended to look inside Knox's notebook, but the boring bus ride, a desperate need to avoid my own depressing thoughts, and my overwhelming curiosity were a lethal combination, and within seconds my fingers were itching to open its pages. I glanced around again at the passengers around me, like they'd somehow know I was snooping. But of course no one was paying me any attention. I took a deep breath and unthreaded the little leather tie securing the book, then opened the book slowly, as if it held a great secret that I wanted to savor.

Inside the pages was anything but what I expected. Outside it looked like a journal, but there were no journal entries. Just sketch after sketch of the same woman. She was incredibly lifelike and beautiful with long dark hair curled in soft tendrils around her shoulders, wide yet sad eyes, and a graceful neck that led to a delicate collarbone. The simple pencil sketches with smudges of gray and black against the stark whiteness of the page gave the drawings a gritty, realistic feeling.

I could almost see Knox bent over this notebook, pencil in hand, a furrow of concentration slashed between his eyebrows. I wondered who the woman was. A former lover? His girlfriend? For the first time, I wondered about the man beyond his sexual addiction. I knew from my training that a sexual addition was often masking some other issue. With Knox, I had no idea what that might be. He seemed healthy and in control. But perhaps that was just a mask he put on.

I was so engrossed in the sketches that when the bus rolled to a stop, I barely noticed. Startled by other passengers rising and exiting the bus, I quickly wrapped the notebook with its leather ties and joined them when I realized it was my stop.

Huddling into my jacket for warmth, I walked through the neighborhood, noting the older homes, likely built in the early 1900s. Most were in need of a fresh coat of paint, and some needed a whole lot more—new windows, a replacement roof, or even a bulldozer.

When I found the house that bore his address, I stopped and looked up at the three-story home to see peeling pale yellow paint, a slanted front porch, and a heavy wooden door. It should have looked cold and uninviting, but some unspecified characteristic gave it charm. It felt homey and inviting, even if it was a strange home for a guy who appeared to be in his early twenties. Maybe he shared the big space with several roommates.

Clutching the leather-bound notebook in my hands, I climbed up the front steps and knocked on the door. Voices sounded from inside, but no one came. I waited several long moments and knocked again, more firmly this time.

A young boy with messy dark hair answered the door. "Hi," he said simply, his smile revealing two missing front teeth.

"Hi. Um, is Knox here?" I asked uncertainly, all traces of confidence vanishing.

"Uh-huh." He turned from the front door, leaving it wide open, presumably for me to follow him inside. With my heart slamming nervously into my ribs, I crossed the threshold and followed the little boy, sensing that everything I thought I knew was about to be challenged.

The scene in front of me took a moment to process. Knox was holding a baby girl in his arms and two teenage boys were wrestling on the living room couch. With all the commotion, they'd yet to notice me.

Knox looked completely at ease with the baby resting in his strong arms, and she was happily engrossed watching the wrestling match, blowing bubbles and cooing at the sight. I took all this in within a matter of seconds, trying to place what exactly I was seeing.

All three boys looked like mini versions of Knox. Dark hair, soulful caramel-colored eyes, and all of them were tall. Even the little boy who'd answered the door nearly reached my height of five foot two. But the baby had me baffled. She had light golden-blonde hair that hung in tiny ringlets around her face and big bright blue eyes.

Knox and the other guys still hadn't noticed me, and the little boy who'd answered the door had busied himself with a giant pile of Legos in the center of the living room floor, while the others continued arguing. I took the opportunity to glance around at the rooms around me. The house was decorated with mismatched furnishings that had seen better days. But it was cozy and fairly neat. A large blue couch sat atop a woven brown rug and was flanked by wooden end tables scattered with papers and a baby bottle. A set of shelves held an array of toys and books, and straight ahead I could see the kitchen and dining room, along with a set of stairs that went off to my right. The home felt lived-in, not at all like my cramped, industrial-feeling apartment where everything was beige.

"Luke, Jaxon, cool it, would you? Grab me a diaper and some wipes," Knox said, hoisting the baby up higher in his grasp.

"Oh fuck. Do you smell that?" The taller of the two boys rose to his feet, sniffing the air. "We've got a code green!"

"Don't curse around Bailee, you dipshit." The slightly shorter boy rose from the couch and shoved the other in the shoulder.

I cleared my throat and four sets of expressive brown eyes swung over to mine.

"McKenna?" Knox asked, his eyebrows rising. "What are you doing here?"

A bundle of nerves rose in my stomach and lodged in my throat. The grand plan I'd hatched about coming here to face him suddenly felt immature and idiotic. He had his own life and responsibilities, and here I was tracking him down like a schoolgirl with a crush.

"I—" My voice squeaked and I started again. "I just wanted to apologize for earlier." I held up his notebook. "And return this to you."

His eyes searched mine and his face softened. The little girl in his arms let out a short cry, pulling our gazes apart. "It's okay, baby girl." He bounced the little thing on his hip to quiet her like he'd done it a million times before.

"These are my brothers. Tucker." He pointed to the little boy on the floor. "Jaxon and Luke." Jaxon was the next tallest after Knox, probably six feet and had longish hair that hung in his eyes, and Luke was just a fraction shorter. "And this is Bailee." He looked down at the little girl in his arms, but offered no further explanation.

"Guys, will one of you change Bailee so McKenna and I can go talk?"

"Hi, I'm Luke." The shorter boy offered me his hand and I shook it. His entire hand closed around mine. I'd guess that he and Jaxon were both in high school, and I also guessed with their thick hair and gorgeous eyes fringed in dark lashes, they were both popular with the girls. Just like their older brother.

"Hi, Luke. It's nice to meet you."

"Who are you?" Jaxon asked, his mouth in a crooked grin as he looked me up and down.

"I'm a…friend of your brother's."

"Knox doesn't have friends who are girls," he challenged.

My mouth hung open. I was clueless about how to respond.

Knox stepped between us. "Enough, guys. Go take care of Bailee." After handing the baby off to Luke, Knox turned to fully face me. I took in his chest-hugging thermal tee, dark denim, and bare feet. It was a side of him I wouldn't have guessed at. Softer, paternal. It made my stomach tighten. I was used to things in my life being neat and orderly; I liked knowing what to expect. Knox challenged everything I thought I knew, and left me wanting to piece it all together.

"Join me in the kitchen?" he asked.

"Sure." I waited for him to lead the way. I should have felt intimidated around him, with his broad shoulders and height, but I didn't. Seeing him around his brothers made me feel completely comfortable.

His jaw tensed as he noticed the boys still watching us. "On second thought, there's too many little ears down here. Are you okay if we go upstairs?" His dark honey eyes latched on to mine and I was rendered speechless. Join him in his bedroom? I should probably say no. But my head bobbed up and down in a nod.

Knox motioned me in front of him and I started up the stairs.

I could feel his hot gaze on my backside the entire way up the stairs. I wanted to spin around and catch him looking, but then what would I say? *Like what you see?* I wasn't that brazen, so I continued climbing while my body heated under his stare that I could feel all the way to my core.

When we reached the second floor, his hand went to my lower back with a feather-light touch to silently guide me, indicating that I should continue up the third flight of stairs to the attic. From the way his fingertips lightly raked against my spine, I could tell he knew his way around a woman's body. The thought both excited and frustrated me. How many women had he led up these stairs in the exact same manner?

I desperately needed to keep my perspective about why I was here. To help him as a member of my group. That was all. *Right, McKenna, that's why you haven't stopped thinking about him once…and bussed it across the city just to return a notebook.*

When we reached the third floor, the wooden planks

creaked as I crossed the large bedroom, light streaming in on both sides from dormer windows set deeply into the vaulted ceiling. His bedroom was set up more like a mini apartment, with a sofa and TV on one side of the room, and queen-sized bed at the far end where the ceilings pitched their lowest.

I couldn't help but notice the half-empty bottle of whiskey on his bedside table, and the hole punched through the wall a few feet from his bed. A pang of unease about being up here alone with him sliced right through my middle. I didn't know him. Not at all. Yet here I was, alone in his bedroom. I'd never been so reckless and inquisitive, but something about Knox's quiet intensity pushed me outside my comfort zone. I wanted to learn everything there was to know about this troubled, beautiful man.

He motioned me over to the sofa and I sat down, my back straight as an arrow with the notebook resting in my lap. I wondered if his bedroom was where Knox took his conquests. I knew the darker side of this addiction and the impulsive behaviors that drove people to sex in public restrooms, alleyways, backseats of cars, and all sorts of strange places. But I didn't like the idea that Knox's attic bedroom, where I currently sat with him, might also be the place he lost himself in other women.

"Relax, McKenna," he whispered and smiled before sitting down across from me in an old leather armchair.

I released a silent exhale and handed him the notebook. "You left this."

He took it from my hands, his thumb brushing mine and sending a small thrill up my arm. "Thanks." He waited, silently watching me, like he knew if he just waited me out, I would explain what I was really doing here.

I took my time, looking around the room, from the gray sheets that were tangled on his bed to a little desk that sat in the corner, complete with a stack of unpaid bills. My unease about Knox, about his life obviously so very different from my own, ratcheted a little higher.

"Did you look inside?" he asked, looking down at the journal in his hands.

"No," I blurted too quickly, my face flushing with heat. We both knew it was a hasty lie.

He untied the leather string fastened around the notebook and opened the pages to me, turning the book so I could see. He glanced up to watch my reaction, and I brought my hand to the open page, lightly tracing the shadows he'd captured so realistically under her wide eyes. She looked tired and so lifelike.

"You're very talented," I murmured. "She must be someone important to you."

"My mother," he confirmed.

I met his eyes and smiled. He clearly loved his mother to devote so many hours to sketching her likeness. He flipped through a few of the pages for me to see, and then set the book on the table between us. Again, he waited for me to fill the silence.

My curiosity was too much. "So, Bailee's your…" I left him to fill in the blank.

"Neighbor's daughter. We babysit her sometimes for Nikki while she works. Plus it's probably good for her to have some male role models since her dad's not in the picture."

"Oh."

Knox cracked a lopsided grin. "You thought she was mine?"

"I wasn't sure. You seemed pretty comfortable with her."

He shrugged. "I guess I am. I mean, I'm comfortable around kids. I have three younger brothers I helped raise. And Bailee's here enough. She's a pretty easy baby."

"Except for that code green stuff?"

He shrugged. "It's good for the guys to learn to change diapers and warm up bottles. It teaches them responsibility."

"So you all live here…with your parents?" My voice rose on the question.

"Mom passed away seven years ago, and my dad took off with a waitress a few years after that. I have custody of the boys."

"Oh." Everything I thought I knew about Knox, the sex-addicted playboy, was lost in that instant. He was a man who worked hard and loved his family enough to step up and provide for them, putting his own dreams and goals aside. He was a real person, not just one of the bodies who filled a chair at my little group Saturday mornings. And now that I'd gotten a glimpse, I wanted to know more.

"So…" I looked around his room, my uncertainty about being here obvious. "This is your life."

"This is it," he confirmed. "Not what you expected?"

His raising his brothers and babysitting for a neighbor? No. Not at all. I glanced to his bedside table again, my eyes seeking the bottle of amber-colored liquor that sat there. I wondered what demons lurked just under the surface of his controlled demeanor. Why he needed the vices he did.

Perhaps we had more similarities than I realized. We were both on our own without our parents. Knox's load of responsibility was heavier than mine, but my guilt over how I lost my parents might have made up for that deficit. We were each wise beyond our years, burdened with things at a young age. Maybe we recognized that in each other. Something to draw us together. Because I certainly felt drawn to him. More than anyone.

Annoyed, I gave myself a mental kick in the pants, forcing myself to remember I was here to help him, not to pry into every facet of his life.

"Why won't you open up in group, Knox?" When he shrugged and made a non-committal noise in his throat, I pushed a little harder. "What are you afraid of?"

His gaze leapt to mine. "I'm not afraid. I'm just private. I don't particularly want to air my dirty laundry in front of a bunch of strangers. Can you blame me?"

"That's a very normal feeling. But most people find that once they cross that hurdle and open up, there's a certain comfort in knowing there are others out there with the same struggles. You're not alone, Knox. The first step is just admitting you have a problem."

My little speech was met with silence while Knox looked deep in thought. "How about this...I'll tell you some things that you want to know, if you'll do the same."

"You want to know about me?" I asked, surprise evident in my voice.

He shrugged. "Fair's fair."

If that would get him talking, I didn't see any harm. "I'm game. Who starts?"

"I do." Knox's dark eyes searched mine, and I fought a little shiver that prickled the skin at the back of my neck. "How did you become a sex addict counselor? Do you have experience with addiction yourself?" Interest flickered in his gaze.

I chewed on my lip again. The story was nothing as dark or interesting as that. The truth was the grief counselor I began seeing in high school led me down this path.

"I went to school for counseling and after I graduated with my bachelor's degree, I took a part-time position at a center for troubled teens here in the city. I had extra time, so I looked into what other opportunities I could get involved in, and I got linked up with this lady Belinda. She leads SAA and became my mentor. Then after a while of sitting in with her groups, I got my own group."

Sheesh, I was rambling, but something about the intent way Knox watched me while I spoke, looking between my mouth and my eyes, left me distracted and warm. I drew a deep breath, trying to clear my head. Knox was still watching me, waiting for me to ask him something. It was my turn.

"So…" I drew out the word, buying time. I could go for the obvious, asking him how he ended up with this addiction, but something told me not to push him. I wanted him to open up and feel comfortable, so I couldn't interrogate him from the start. I liked talking to him and I wasn't ready for it to end. "Tell me about your brothers," I said at last.

Knox leaned back into the armchair, crossing one ankle over his knee. Gosh, he was so big, so male, that it was impossible not to notice how completely he filled the small space between us. My pulse jumped and quickened in response.

"Tucker's eight and in the third grade. He's a good kid, listens to his teachers, and keeps his room clean." He released a heavy sigh. "He has an amazing capacity for love. He was so little when we lost her and when Dad took off, that I think he's the least affected by it."

Listening to him talk made me wonder what the little boy had been through. I couldn't imagine losing my mom at such a tender age, and then having to watch my dad run off and abandon the family. My heart ached for him.

"Luke is seventeen and he's a junior. He's smart. Like *smart*-smart. He wants to go to college and he studies hard so he can qualify for a scholarship when the time comes. And Jaxon…" He shook his head. "Jaxon is too much like I was. He's eighteen and will graduate in the spring. I thought I'd feel relieved once he turned eighteen, knowing that he could ensure the boys didn't get split up if something ever happened to me…"

He hesitated, and something in his eyes made me sad. I could see how much he worried about them.

"I'm sure he'd step up if he needed to," he went on.

72

"But for now, he has no plan of what to do when he graduates, no job, no money, and he chases after girls just like I did at that age."

It surprised me how much Knox was sharing. As uncertain as I'd felt, I was glad I'd followed my instincts and came here today. Maybe he just needed someone to talk to. Not that I'd been thinking about my background in counseling a moment ago. I'd been thinking about his sad eyes, and the way my heart slammed into my ribs when he was near.

Knox grew quiet, like he'd said too much. His eyes slowly lifted to mine. "Your turn, angel."

KNOX

Something about seeing McKenna in my space was surreal. I couldn't believe she was actually here, sitting in my bedroom. My messy-ass bedroom.

When she'd refused my offer for coffee, I'd seen the momentary indecision in her eyes. She'd wanted to say yes. But something had kept her from acting on it. So I'd left my notebook behind on the table, wondering if would propel her to find me. She had. And now she wanted me to spill my secrets, to psychoanalyze me. Too bad. I wasn't opening up until she did the same. I didn't know shit about this girl; I didn't have to tell her anything. She wasn't my court-appointed counselor. But if she took the first step, showed me I could trust her, I wasn't opposed to talking. Something about her intrigued me.

And now, after just a few minutes, I was sitting here spilling my guts like a pussy. I needed to switch us to a lighter topic. She wanted to be let in, but I was pretty sure she'd hate me once she really knew all of it.

Her back was still ramrod straight and she totally looked out of place. It was adorable and struck something inside me. I wanted to see her pretty, unsure smile again. "Is your boyfriend going to be mad you came here?" I asked with the hint of a smile playing on my lips. Her denying that he was her boyfriend would definitely make the alpha male in me happy.

"Brian?" Her brows pulled together. "He's just a friend."

"No boyfriend then?"

She shook her head. "No. No boyfriend. What about you?"

"I prefer females. I thought we'd established that was my main problem." Her cheeks flushed ever so slightly. "And no, angel, I don't have a girlfriend."

"Knox," she started, then stopped herself, chewing on her lower lip before continuing. "I'm sorry I'm here taking up your time, I just came to apologize for how I reacted today. I thought you were blowing off the group and trying to pick me up."

That might have been my intention at the time, but now it was anything but. McKenna wasn't like the girls I was used to. If I pressured her into going out with me, something told me I'd only push her away. And I wasn't ready for that to happen.

"I was serious about being more comfortable talking one-on-one versus in a roomful of people."

She nodded. "I get that. I'm sorry again. I figured it was a come-on."

I shook my head. "Not my intention, angel."

She frowned, like the idea that I wasn't coming on to her was a slight disappointment. This girl just got more and more interesting the more time I spent with her. I shifted in the chair so I was leaning a little closer to McKenna. Her scent was light and crisp, with the warmth of vanilla and a hint of soap. Not too overpowering, but subtle and pleasant. Just like the girl herself.

The stairs creaked and I glanced over to see Tucker peeking around the corner to spy on us. I'd purposefully left my bedroom door open; I didn't want any confusion over what was happening between me and McKenna.

"Would you like to stay for lunch?" I asked her. A healthy relationship with a female might be just the kind of normal thing my brothers needed to see from me. And after Jaxon's wise-ass comment that *Knox doesn't have friends who are girls*, I wanted to show them I did. Or at least I could.

McKenna met my eyes and nodded uncertainly. "Okay. That sounds…nice."

"Cool. But you have to help me cook."

She smiled warmly at me, a smile too nice and genuine for someone like me, and I felt a stab of regret about luring her into my world. Something in me wanted her, and that was very dangerous.

Downstairs, we found the guys rummaging through the cabinets and munching on handfuls of crackers and chips.

"McKenna's staying for lunch." I urged them to put the junk food away and motioned for McKenna to have a seat up on the counter while I gathered ingredients for spaghetti. It was a staple meal around here—inexpensive, easy, and filling. I piled a box of pasta, a jar of sauce, and a package of ground beef on the counter, then grabbed a skillet from the cabinet between McKenna's legs. She gasped at the unexpected invasion and I rose to my feet, smiling innocently.

77

"So, how do you know Knox?" Luke asked, looking back and forth between the two of us.

As she paused, obviously struggling to answer his question. "I met her at group," I interrupted, and she tossed me a grateful smile. I took the opportunity to study her again. Even I had to admit there was something about McKenna that seemed out of place in my life. She was wearing dark jeans that hugged her ass nicely, a white button-down shirt that looked really soft, and little diamond earrings. She looked sweet and wholesome.

Looking down at myself, I took in my worn jeans, a faded black T-shirt, and socks with a hole in the toe. My brothers were no better off. Most of their clothes were secondhand too. Not that we minded; we had what we needed. Something told me McKenna came from money, but I also had the sense she was more than okay slumming here with us. I just wished I knew why. Was she running from something in her life too?

After we ate, the guys headed outside to play basketball, and McKenna and I settled on the living room sofa together. She was different than I would have guessed—not at all stuck-up. She'd laughed and joked with my brothers while eating a big helping of my spaghetti, which was little more than overcooked noodles and runny tomato sauce, and then had helped with the dishes. And now she was sitting cross-legged on my couch looking delectable as fuck. The desire to kiss her shot through me like an arrow.

Knowing I couldn't do a thing about it was a special kind of torture.

"It's getting dark," Knox commented, looking toward the front windows.

Following his gaze, I noted the way the late-afternoon sun was sinking into the horizon, leaving the sky with an eerie glow. "Are you worried about the boys being out after dark?"

"No. They'll be fine." He was quiet for a moment, but still looked lost in his thoughts. "When night comes and everything is quiet…" He paused, reluctant to continue. I waited, holding my breath and hoping that he'd open up to me. "I realize it's just me, with all this pressure riding on me, and I need someone. Some company to make me feel whole again." He cleared his throat and looked down at his hands.

I didn't like nighttime either, but I wanted to know more about what he meant. "Is that why you go out at night?" I ventured.

"I need that place where I become numb to the world

and can forget everything for a little while," he admitted, his gaze still fixed on the fading afternoon sun.

He was actually letting me in. Even if it was just a peek, seeing inside the mind of this man was like opening a window and sucking in a deep breath of fresh air. It was enlightening.

Nights were the hardest for me too. I wondered if that was part of the reason I found myself here, reluctant to go home. In the darkness, my guilt was its thickest. I lay in bed and thought about my parents, and the feelings of guilt and despair almost drowned me. But I'd never considered throwing myself at a man to make me forget. Volunteering was my escape. I lost myself in the servitude of others. I used their problems and misfortunes to remind myself that people out there had it worse. Perhaps Knox and I weren't so different, after all. He just medicated himself in a very different way.

He turned back to face me, his dark gaze deep and penetrating. We watched each other for several heartbeats while delicious tension swirled between us. I wondered what had happened to lead him here. I knew he'd lost his mother, and his father had left, but how had he become this lust-filled version of himself?

Watching his sad eyes, I thought I understood what he was saying about the darkness. It was the same feeling that haunted me. I didn't have bills and siblings to worry about, but my parents' deaths had left a hole in my heart. I couldn't stand to be alone with my grief, so I threw myself into work. Knox threw himself into the arms of women. We forced our pain away by chasing after distractions. Sleeping around was his version of my volunteering.

"Sorry, that was probably a weird thing to say." He shook his head, as if trying to clear the thoughts.

I wanted to take his hand, but instead my hand came to a stop beside his, not quite touching, but sending my message all the same. He hadn't pushed me away. And I wanted him to know I appreciated it, and that we shared more than he knew.

Turning to face me yet again, Knox's voice dropped lower, taking on a serious tone. "Are you sure it was wise coming here? Hanging out with me alone?"

"Why wouldn't it be?"

He swallowed, his lips moving in a distracting way. "I'm a sex addict."

My heart sped up as his words ricocheted through

me. "Should I be afraid of you?"

"I wouldn't hurt you, but that doesn't mean I don't want to do some other things."

"L-like what other things?" I unconsciously leaned closer, drawn forward by his magnetism.

Knox let out a low, throaty chuckle and leaned back against the couch, stared straight up at the ceiling, and let out a heavy exhale. "Oh, McKenna." He patted my head like I was a naive little girl.

Maybe I was foolish and naive for coming here today, but I could handle myself. It wasn't like I was at risk for falling for this man, was I?

The trio of boys burst in through the front door, ending our strained silence. I could tell that Knox was as pleased as I was at their timing. Knox scooted further away from me on the sofa to make room for the littlest, Tucker, and soon we were in an intense racing game on their Xbox. They all took turns beating me and laughing at the way my entire body moved as I tried to steer my race car.

I had stayed at Knox's far longer than I'd intended, nearly five hours. The time had flown by, laughing and eating with him and his brothers. I hadn't felt this relaxed and happy in a long time.

By the time darkness fell, it was pouring down rain outside. I was going to be soaked through by the time I made it home, but I had to suck it up. Somehow I knew calling Brian for a ride would be a bad idea. He'd never approve of my being at Knox's.

Reluctantly, I stood up. "I guess I should get going."

"All right." Knox stood next to me and crossed his arms over his chest. "Are you parked out front? I can walk you out." Before I could answer, he grabbed an umbrella from a closet by the front door.

I slowly turned to face him. "No, I don't have a car. I took the bus here."

A crease appeared between Knox's brows. "You took the city bus here?"

I nodded.

"Guys, I'll be back soon," he said, turning to address his brothers. "Come on, I'm driving you home. There's no way I'm letting you ride the bus after dark."

Letting me? He had a commanding way with words, but it had been a long time since I felt concern as genuine as Knox's seemed to be. Even if it was unexpected, it was nice.

The interior of Knox's Jeep smelled like him—sandalwood and warm leather. We rode the few miles to my apartment building while I pointed out the directions. I liked watching him drive. His long fingers curled around the wheel as his denim-covered thighs stretched out before him, drawing my eyes.

When Knox pulled to a stop outside the building, I wasn't ready to go. Reading my hesitation, he turned to face me. "Should I walk you up? Make sure everything's safe?"

"No, that's okay. Brian's home." I pointed to the black sedan parked three spaces down.

"Brian's that guy who came to your meeting to pick you up?"

I nodded.

"You live with him."

It wasn't a question, but I could see the uncertainty in his eyes. "Yes, but he's just a friend, my roommate."

"Are you fucking him?"

"N-no," I choked out. Suddenly I felt hot and

uncomfortable in the small, dark space with Knox, off-balance at the abrupt change in his tone. Why would he care if I was sleeping with Brian or not? "Do you have a date tonight?" I asked.

"I don't date."

I swallowed. "Fine. Will you be requiring company later?"

"Yes." His dark gazed pierced mine, looking hungry and full of desire. "I can't be expected to watch you parade around in your tight jeans all night and not need a release."

It was the first time he'd mentioned that my physical appearance had an effect on him. And I'd be lying if I said I didn't like it. God, what was wrong with me? He needed help, not another girl throwing herself at him. Besides, I should feel disgusted; he had just admitted he was going out looking for sex after spending the evening with me.

"Good night, McKenna," he said, his tone final and dismissive.

"Good night." I climbed from the Jeep, sliding from the seat until both feet touched the ground. Without looking back I headed inside, the cool rain a balm against my warm, flushed face.

Chapter Nine

It had been a week since I'd seen Knox. Never in my life had I looked forward to my Saturday morning group so much.

All week I replayed in my mind the time we spent together at his house. I had felt a pull inside me, an indescribable urge to get closer to him. There were so many layers to his personality, so many sides to him. I wanted to know each one, to turn him like a crystal in the light, to inspect his many facets.

Knox entered the room and a slow smile tugged at my mouth. With his messy dark hair sticking up in several directions, he looked like he'd just rolled out of bed. He was dressed in jeans, work boots left unlaced, and a plain white T-shirt with a gray wool jacket slung over his arm. He looked rugged and beautiful. His eyes cut straight to mine. The way he looked at me was overwhelming; I could feel that penetrating gaze deep inside my body. And I liked it way too much.

I all but collapsed into my chair, needing to sit to steady my nerves. That week's group session was about making amends for your past wrongs. Basically it was about getting right with yourself and others in order to move forward.

We spent much of the hour talking about sexually transmitted diseases, how to notify past lovers of bad news, and the courage that took. A few people already had recent tests completed, and spoke about how nerve-wracking it was to get their results. Most of the others agreed to get testing done, and we agreed to talk next time about how to handle whatever their outcomes might be. I had the contact information for an AIDS/HIV support group at my desk, but I hoped I didn't need it. Thinking like that was probably juvenile, though. These people had exposed themselves and others to serious risk, and I feared theirs might not all be good news.

Throughout the entire conversation, Knox was quiet and contemplative as always. I wondered about his status and if he'd also pursue the testing this week. Something told me probably not. At least, not without a little shove.

I ended the group by passing out information on the local clinics that offered free testing. Knox took the flyer, but stuffed it inside his jacket pocket without reading it.

After everyone else had filtered out of the room, Knox stood and stretched, his arms lifting above his head. The movement lifted his T-shirt several inches to expose firm, sculpted abs. A bolt of heat raced through me. I really needed to have this thermostat checked.

I wandered over to where he stood, summoning my courage. "Have you been tested?"

His eyes flashed on mine, seemingly surprised I'd questioned him so directly. "I always use condoms."

I felt a small measure of comfort knowing that information. Of course it wasn't enough, but it was something. "Condoms can break. You should be tested."

"I have no weird symptoms. No burning sensation when I pee. I'm good." He smiled, trying to turn this into something lighthearted, but I stood my ground.

"You have your brothers to think about, Knox. Do it for them." It might have been an unfair move, playing his brothers against him, but I knew that would get through.

He pulled the rumpled flyer from his pocket and looked down at it. "Come with me?" he asked, his voice barely above a whisper.

"Of course."

His eyes lifted to meet mine. "Now?"

I hesitated, then relented. "Okay."

We waited at the clinic almost an hour before they could see Knox. They were busy on Saturdays, but still, I was glad we were here. I worried that if we postponed this, he'd never come back. He'd tried to encourage me to get tested too, handing me a clipboard when we checked in, but I'd refused. Little did Knox know, my sexual past was all but nonexistent. We were quite opposites in that way.

When he emerged from the doctor's office fifteen minutes later, his expression was sour, and his posture tense. "Let's go." He didn't bother stopping to wait for me to put my coat back on, so I jogged after him, stuffing my arms into the jacket as I tried to catch up.

"What happened?"

He turned to face me once we'd reached his Jeep in the parking lot. "I did it, all right?"

"Well, what's wrong?" I knew he wouldn't get his results for a week, so I was clueless about his sour mood.

"They jammed a giant Q-tip up my dick."

I giggled, relieved that it wasn't something worse. "I'm sure you'll live."

"You think that's funny?" The line between his brow softened as he looked me over.

I put on a straight face. "Sorry. No. I just…I'm glad you did this."

"Come on, I'm taking you home. Besides, I'm sure you're off to do more good in the world after this."

I didn't argue and climbed inside the Jeep, happy with my little breakthrough with him. Today had been a victory and I felt proud, though more than a little worried about his results.

Chapter Ten

Later that week when I arrived home from the teen shelter, I was absolutely starving since I'd missed lunch. I pulled open the fridge and surveyed its disappointing contents. Brian's micro-brew beer, margarine, and a bag of baby carrots that were starting to petrify.

My parents had left me money. I didn't have to live this way, rooming with Brian, buying just the bare essentials and going without a car, but up to this point, I'd refused to give in. I wanted to be stronger than that, to stand on my own two feet and not use the blood money from their life insurance policies or my father's pension. It would feel like cheating and only twist the knife deeper in my chest to have to rely on that money.

And so far, I'd made it. Chicago was far more expensive than I'd anticipated and my meager salary didn't go far. But even if that meant my diet was mainly peanut butter and jelly sandwiches and forgoing a new coat this winter, it was worth it. Some days I thought about donating it all to one of the charities I loved, but something always held me back. My parents worked hard for what they had. They would have wanted me to have it. So I left it in a trust, just in case. But I hoped I was never desperate enough to touch it.

Abandoning the fridge to scan the cupboards didn't provide much in the way of options either. I needed to get to the store soon. It was times like this I missed my mom. She was an amazing cook and would have whipped me up something delicious from the simplest of ingredients. That was her talent. It didn't matter if all we had was boxed pasta and shredded cheese. I'd have an amazing hot meal in front of me in minutes. Before I could decide what to do, Brian came in behind me.

"Come sit down, McKenna." His voice was commanding and I wondered what was on his mind. I'd paid my share of the rent, and had even remembered to mail the electric bill on time this month.

I sat down on the sofa and Brian lowered himself down next to me.

"Are you doing okay?"

I fidgeted under his watchful stare. "Fine. Just a little tired. It was a long week."

"You work too hard. You're always running, always on the go. It doesn't have to be this way."

I blinked at him, wondering what had inspired his little speech. "I like staying busy, you know that." It helped me. I would hate to think what I'd do with an entire day alone with my thoughts. I shuddered at the idea.

"I'm your family now." Brian's hand came to rest on my knee.

I no longer had a family. Brian might be a nice guy, but he didn't feel like family. Sure, we'd grown up together and I was totally comfortable around him, even in my holey sweatpants and my mom's ratty old slippers. But something was missing. It wasn't his shoulder I wanted to lean on when things got tough. The image of Knox cradling baby Bailee against his shoulder rushed into my brain. She'd rested her head on him and let out the softest little sigh. I hadn't felt that kind of comfort in ages.

"I could take care of you, McKenna. My job pays enough, you could stop working around the clock. You could just be happy."

I stared at him, dumbfounded. Happy? How could I ever be happy not working? And I certainly didn't do it for the money. Most of my hours were unpaid volunteer work.

94

Brian didn't really know me at all if he thought that. His words reminded me that I had no one, no family, and a rush of wetness filled my eyes. Perhaps it was because I was starving and bone tired, but I couldn't handle this conversation right now. Silent tears threatened to overflow, so I excused myself to the bathroom where I could cry alone like the loser I was.

Ignoring Brian's hurt expression, I scurried away and shut myself in the small room. I locked the door firmly behind me, then closed the toilet lid and sank down. I had spent all day pretending everything was fine, that I was in control, but one tiny conversation about the current state of my life and I broke down, sobbing like a baby.

I'd taken my parents for granted, but now that they were gone, I realized just how much they meant to me. I was an only child, their miracle baby, since they were told they'd never have kids. It broke my heart even more for them. All the years of struggle, all they went through to have me, and I was so oblivious, totally ungrateful and self-centered in the years before they died. A voice of reason chimed in, reminding me a lot of teens were that way, but I forced the thought away. I deserved to feel every bit as sad and lonely as I was in that moment.

I wiped the tears away with the back of my hand and grabbed a wad of toilet paper to blow my nose. All day I had been cheerful and helpful, fixing a brave face firmly in place as I helped others. But the harsh truth was that I was totally and completely helpless.

Watching Knox interact with his brothers only reinforced what I already knew. Family was everything. Without one, I felt like I didn't fit in anywhere. And definitely not here in Chicago, with Brian as my only friend and pseudo family.

The crazy thing was, when I was near Knox that painful ache in my chest vanished. It was like his presence alone had some strange impact on me. I could stop worrying and planning my next move. I could just *be*. It was a feeling of total relief. Maybe the craziness of his life balanced out my own. He certainly had a lot on his plate and a truckload of issues to work through. Those were things I recognized. They made sense to me.

I was struck by the sudden realization that I wanted to see him. I wanted to spend time with him and his brothers. I wanted the distraction and company they provided. Their loud, messy household and camaraderie. A pang of guilt hit me as I realized it was for entirely selfish reasons, but I didn't care. Not enough to keep me away from him.

Making a plan in my head, I blew my nose one more time and splashed cool water on my cheeks. I straightened my shoulders and leaned over to inspect myself in the mirror, only to see splotchy pink marks had discolored my cheeks and neck, and my eyes were rimmed in red. *Crap*.

I dabbed on some concealer and ran a brush through my hair. If I was going to catch them before they made other plans for dinner, I needed to get moving and go buy some groceries.

By the time I left the grocery store, the sky was a pretty pink color as the sun was starting its descent. I was hopeful and excited for the first time that week.

Guilt had stabbed me as I'd lied to Brian about where I was headed, but something told me he wouldn't have taken the news well that I was going to Knox's. The label of *sex addict* was enough to immediately dissuade him from liking Knox. I was willing to suspend judgment. There seemed to be so many more sides to him.

I didn't even notice the cooling night air. A bit of chill would do nothing to dampen my mood as I strolled purposefully toward Knox's place. I hadn't realized how badly I'd needed to see him after lusting after him these last several days.

Anticipation gave me a little rush as I climbed the steps leading up to his house, balancing a big bag of groceries on my hip. I'd gotten a package of chicken, potatoes, bread, frozen peas, and a cake mix too, hoping it would be enough to feed all the boys. I briefly wondered if they were watching Bailee again, and imagined Knox smashing up some of the peas and potatoes for her dinner. Was she even big enough to eat vegetables yet?

As I started up the steps, it occurred to me how dark the house was. There were no lights burning inside and a pang of nerves hit me. I didn't know what I'd do if they weren't home. My entire mood hinged on getting to see Knox tonight. Not healthy, I know.

I knocked twice and rang the bell, but the house remained utterly silent. My stomach sank to my toes as I waited, hoping someone would answer. The tears from earlier threatened to make another appearance as bitter disappointment coursed through me. No one was home. I wondered if Knox was out with a girl right now and the idea stung.

A commotion in the street caught my attention and I

turned. Knox and the two younger boys strolled up the street, cheering and hollering and generally being rambunctious boys. My heart jumped at the sight of Knox balancing three large pizza boxes in one hand, and Tucker hoisted up on his shoulder.

"McKenna?" Knox set Tucker on his feet and stopped directly in front of me. His large form overwhelmed me and even though I'd been hungry to see him, I now found myself a little unsure about showing up here unannounced again. "Is everything okay?" he asked, inspecting me from head to toe.

I liked the way his gaze slid over me way too much. He saw the real me, the one I hid from everyone else. He knew I wasn't here for anything related to the group. I was here because I wanted to be.

Knowing he could read my expression—I never did have much of a poker face—I lifted my mouth in a smile and held up the bag of groceries. "I came to make dinner." My gaze floated over to the pizza boxes he was holding.

"Tucker won his soccer game. We're celebrating with his favorite—ham and pineapple pizza. You're welcome to join us." His eyes appraised me coolly, as if waiting to see what I'd do.

"I…I don't know."

"Come on, who can say no to pizza?" He grinned and waved the boxes tantalizingly in front of me.

He was right, my stomach grumbled at the scent. Pizza with Knox and his brothers sounded perfect right now. Much better than taking the bus back home alone and sitting there with Brian watching me all night while he pretended to be working on his laptop.

"That'd be great." I hoisted the bag of groceries on my hip, immediately feeling better as my previous disappointment faded into the background.

"What's all that?" Knox tipped his head to the bag while unlocking the front door.

"I was, um…" *Spit it out, McKenna.* "Going to make you guys dinner. Sort of as a thank-you for inviting me to eat with you last time."

Knox's smile lit up his whole face. He peeked inside the bag. "You'll just have to come back another time then to cook this up."

"Deal." I breathed a sigh of relief and followed him inside.

"Jaxon?" Knox called, turning on lights as we crossed

through the living and dining rooms en route to the kitchen. The house was dark and silent. I hadn't guessed that Jaxon was home. He hadn't answered the door when I knocked.

While Knox set the pizza boxes down on the kitchen table, I went with Tucker to grab paper plates, napkins, and drinks from the fridge. I rounded the corner just in time to see Jaxon shuffling a girl out the front door.

"Hey," he said, strolling up to join us at the kitchen table once the girl was gone.

"Who was that?" Luke asked.

"Lila," Jaxon said, offering no further explanation.

Knox didn't look happy; the easygoing attitude he had outside vanished as he turned to face Jaxon. "What the hell are you wearing?" Knox looked down at Jaxon with his eyebrows raised. "Looks like your jeans got into a fight with a lawn mower."

Jaxon's jeans weren't just ripped at the knees, they were practically shredded from the thighs down. I could easily see the print of his plaid boxer shorts. He grinned. "Lila can be a little rough."

"Go change. Throw those away. And I told you, I

don't want girls here when I'm not home."

"Yeah, because you never have girls here, Knox. Your fucking bedroom practically has a revolving door. I'm surprised there's not a sign-up sheet out in the hall."

"Don't curse." Knox stepped closer, his posture tightening.

His eyes flashed to mine and I couldn't help but betray my curiosity. I chewed on my lip, wondering if what Jaxon said was true.

"Go. Change," Knox repeated. It was clear he didn't want Jaxon to say anything else to me.

As if remembering we were supposed to be celebrating Tucker's win, Knox hoisted him onto his shoulder before walking to the table. "You get the first slice, buddy." He slid Tucker into the chair at the head of the table and we all took our seats.

Over slices of pizza, Tucker recounted his victory to Jaxon and me. His entire face lit up when he talked about scoring his first-ever game-winning goal. As he chatted excitedly, Knox's gaze rested on me, watching me as I ate.

A tight knot formed in my throat and I had to remind myself how to swallow. While I sat reminding myself how to properly chew and swallow my food, I realized one thing. Knox was a good distraction.

Miraculously, for hours I hadn't thought about my parents, or my guilt, or my loneliness. Not once. Brian's earlier warning that I needed to get a life came to mind.

Well, this was me, getting a life. I doubted he'd approve of my methods.

KNOX

Having McKenna here was strange, yet felt completely natural at the same time. I needed to keep it together in front of the guys, but I wanted to pull her aside and ask her why she came back.

Once dinner was over, I sent McKenna into the living room to relax while the guys and I cleared the table. This was all new territory for me—but since she was a guest, she shouldn't have to clean up, right?

I carried the now-empty pizza boxes out to the garbage can and leaned against the side of the house, inhaling deep breaths of cool night air. It smelled like rain. I closed my eyes and tried to calm down. Why was she here? I never got rattled around a woman, but things were different with McKenna. Was it because she led the sex addicts group I was part of? No. I didn't think that was it. She made me feel aware and alive in a way I hadn't felt before, challenged things I thought I knew. She'd talked me into getting STD testing done, though I'd been adamant I didn't need it.

I'd be lying if I said I wasn't nervous for the results to arrive. McKenna thought I did the test for my brothers. The truth was that I did it for her, not for some altruistic purpose. I wanted her. Something told me if I pushed her, I could have her. And I'd never expose her to something I picked up from one of my exploits. I just wasn't ready to go there until I knew I could trust myself with her.

When I headed back inside, I found the boys in the kitchen cleaning up and jumped in to lend a hand, welcoming the distraction from the thoughts swirling inside my brain.

"So, what's McKenna doing back here? I thought she was just your counselor," Jaxon asked, looking down as he washed a glass in the sink. It was how guys worked. Sometimes we found it easier to have conversations when our hands were busy.

I bumped his shoulder as I pushed my way in to rinse. "She is. She's just my counselor. But she came to hang out too. That cool with you?"

"Sure. Why should I care?"

I could tell there was more to it than he was letting

on. He'd brought it up for a reason. Maybe he was just curious about my having a normal relationship with a girl. Hell, I was too. I'd repeatedly told my brothers things weren't like that between McKenna and me, but apparently they knew my history with women too well.

"I like her," Luke said as he stuffed the paper plates into the overflowing trash can.

"Me too," Tucker chimed in. "She's nice."

"She's got a nice ass," Jaxon said, smirking down into the dishwater.

Reaching back with a wet hand, I smacked the back of his head lightly. "Don't talk about her ass, dude."

Shit, he was right, though. Earlier when I'd watched her lift up onto her toes to reach the top shelf in the cupboard, her shirt had ridden up, revealing the milky skin of her lower back and a perfectly round ass I wanted to grip in my hands.

I'd fought the urge to walk up behind her and cage her in against the counter, and rub up against her like a dog in heat. It should be illegal to be that hot and be a sex addiction counselor. Seriously, they needed to outlaw that shit.

The guys wouldn't let me help clean up; apparently it was because they wanted to grill Knox about what my appearance here meant. Hearing him say I was just his counselor had stung. I was starting to wonder if I shouldn't have come. Maybe my being here was confusing.

I sat on the couch and flipped on the TV, wondering what to do. I hadn't felt like just his counselor. It had felt like hanging out with a friend. But apparently I needed to stop being delusional.

Soon the boys had finished their chores, and though Jaxon disappeared up the stairs, the others joined me in the living room. Before I knew it, I was surrounded on the couch by boys, Luke on one side and Tucker on the other. Tucker sat motionless, looking up at me in wonder. "You're really pretty," he said. "And you smell good. Like candy and soap."

"Thank you." I tousled his hair, running my fingers through the too-long strands. He was overdue for a haircut, but the look suited him.

He scooted his body closer and yawned. I patted my thigh and he laid his head down in my lap. My heart full, I reached down and pushed his hair back from his forehead, and he released a contented little sigh and closed his eyes. It seemed these boys were hungry for female attention, and it killed me to think they missed their mother so badly they were willing to accept attention from anyone. Even from me, someone they only met a couple of days ago.

After a little while, Knox went to help Tucker to change into his pajamas and brush his teeth, since it was clear he was wiped out from soccer. That left Luke and me still sitting together on the couch while the TV hummed quietly in the background.

Luke glanced over at me from his perch on the sofa, his expression all serious. "So, are you going to help my brother?"

"I'm trying to." I didn't know how much he knew about Knox's addiction. He knew that Knox saw a counselor, but I wasn't sure if he understood the full picture.

"Does that mean you'll be here more often?"

"I hope so."

"Me too."

After several minutes of comfortable silence, Luke looked over at me again. He was always so thoughtful and calm, his scrunched brows and creased forehead had me wondering what was on his mind.

"McKenna? Can I ask you a question?"

I wondered if it was related to my sudden presence in Knox's life. And how I would explain it. "Sure, what's up?"

"It's kind of a private... You know what, never mind. It's stupid."

Now I was even more curious. "You can ask me anything, Luke." If they didn't have regular access to a female in their lives, I wanted to fulfill the role in any way I could.

"Well, I was just wondering. How do you, um, make a girl's first time special?"

Oh my God. He was not asking me this. How the hell would I know, with my utter lack of experience?

Knox had entered the room after putting Tucker to bed and he glanced over at us briefly, acting disinterested, but I could see the tension in his jaw as he plopped into the armchair and pretended not to listen.

My heartbeat ticked in my throat and I fought to maintain slow, even breaths. When I looked up again, I found Knox's eyes locked on mine, looking straight into my soul. I met Luke's gaze again, who was still waiting for an answer.

I gave him a little nod, as if I answered this type of question all the time. "For a girl, her first time is really important. Probably more so than a guy's." My voice was a little shaky and I cleared my throat, starting again. "It's important to make sure she's really ready and not just going along with it or feeling pressured."

Luke nodded, hanging on my every word. I didn't want to encourage him to have sex, but I also didn't want to counsel him too harshly and pretend this type of stuff didn't happen. He was a junior in high school, and many boys and girls his age were already sexually active. I couldn't turn a blind eye to that fact. Just because I wasn't getting any, didn't mean that other people weren't.

"Yeah, I get that," he said. "It's just, it's a lot of pressure on the guy to make it perfect, ya know?"

I smiled at him. It was sweet that he was worried about making it good for the girl. "No one's first time is perfect. Take your time, make sure you're both enjoying yourselves, and have fun. That's the best advice I can give you." It was the only advice I could give him, considering my own first time was over before it even started. I was a twenty-one-year-old virgin. A fact I wasn't necessarily proud of. Sometimes I felt like a freak.

"Okay, that makes sense." The crease in his forehead disappeared.

"Just be yourself, Luke. You're thoughtful and sweet. Oh, and make sure you have protection. And wear it."

"Yes, ma'am." His cheeks reddened slightly. "They give out condoms in health class."

I nodded. Curious, I wanted to ask him who the special girl was, but I thought more questions might make this conversation awkward and I didn't want to pry. "You can always ask me anything, I want you to know that." I smiled at him and patted his knee, all the while mentally cursing myself for implying I'd be around more, when the truth was I had no idea.

"So you know a lot about this sex stuff, huh?"

"Professionally speaking, I suppose so, but I'm not discussing my private life with you."

Luke's face broke into a wide smile. "That's okay, I don't wanna hear about my brother's sex life. Nasty."

"Your brother and I aren't—"

"I know." He smiled. "He likes you, I can tell." His eyes flashed on mine before he hopped up from the couch and retreated down the hallway.

What did that mean? Knox wasn't sleeping with me because he liked me? His logic seemed backward, but instead of trying to solve the puzzle in my head, I lifted my gaze to meet Knox's caramel-colored eyes, which was a big mistake.

I suppressed a hot shudder at the intensity I saw reflected back at me.

KNOX

Fuck me. Listening to McKenna describe her perfect first time was a special kind of torture. My dick rose to attention, hanging on her every word.

She wanted a lover who took his time, and made sure she was enjoying herself? Sign me up! I'd gladly take the job, right fucking now. I wondered if she had enjoyed her first time. Given the chance, I would make sure she came and called out for more.

Even hotter than imagining myself in McKenna's little sex fantasy was watching the way she navigated a tough conversation with ease. I could tell she already cared about my brothers, and that did insane things to me. I had no clue whose virginity Luke was planning to take and honestly I didn't really care as long as he wrapped it up.

But listening to McKenna's advice, knowing she created a bond—a trust—with him to get him to open up, was pretty fucking cool. These kids didn't have a female role model in their lives. I was the closest thing they had to a mom or a dad, and I often did a shitty job of it.

Especially with feelings and emotions. So it made me breathe a little easier knowing that they could rely on McKenna to fill that void. Even if it was just for now.

When Luke took off for his room, her eyes lifted to mine and I was overcome by a tight feeling in my chest as I watched her. Her cheeks were flushed pink and her breathing came in shallow little gasps. She was nervous and I had no idea why.

"I hope that was okay," she said hesitantly. "What I said to Luke. I don't want to overstep my bounds."

I got up from the chair and crossed the room to stand before her. Since it put my groin at her eye level, I was thankful my erection had faded. Even though things were purely platonic between us, there was a certain awareness we seemed to share when in each other's proximity. It grew stronger each time I saw her, and watching her now, seeing how her body responded when I was near, I couldn't help but believe she felt the same. We couldn't keep avoiding this chemistry between us forever.

Looking down at her, I couldn't stop myself from touching her, so I reached down and stroked my thumb along her cheek. Her skin felt incredibly soft, making me wonder if my skin, in contrast, felt rough and calloused to

114

her.

Finally finding my words, I said, "That was amazing. Thank you for talking to him about that."

She looked up at me in silent gratitude and nodded once.

Reluctantly, I let my hand fall away and took a much-needed step back, trying to put some distance between the heat of her body and mine. Having her around, in my space, in these close quarters day after day was starting to become a challenge. I wanted her, but it was more than that—I didn't want to fuck her and move on like I normally did.

This was all uncharted territory for me, and I sensed it was for McKenna too. I needed to proceed with caution if I wanted to have a chance in hell with her. So I took another step back, watching her like she was an unpredictable wild animal I had no clue what to do with.

"What should we do now?" she asked, still looking up at me.

"Help me take down the fort?" I suggested.

I needed to do something to busy my hands before I disappeared into my room to jerk off. The box of tissues beside my bed was getting plenty of action lately.

McKenna's gaze wandered to the tent that was set up in the middle of the den. "Why is there a tent there?"

I shook my head. "Tucker. Bailee was over today and he thought she'd like it, but anytime he put her in there, she cried."

"Gotcha. Well, taking one down is easier than setting it up, right?"

"Right. Come on."

Watching the sway of her ass as she stood and crossed the room did nothing to help clean up my thoughts. I needed to relieve this sexual tension. If not with McKenna, then with someone else. And soon.

We sat side by side, collapsing poles and folding the tent while I thought about what to say to fill the silence that stretched between us. McKenna was concentrating on fitting the tent back into the bag, her tongue pressed into her lower lip as she worked. When she look up and caught me watching, her tongue darted back inside her mouth. I couldn't help but smirk.

When she looked at me, she didn't just look at me. She looked straight into me, like she could see into my soul. I liked being seen for the man I was on the inside, not just the fuck-up everyone saw on the outside. And since McKenna was here, it meant she wasn't judging me based on what she saw.

"Are you going out after this?" she asked, fiddling with the tie on the bag, deliberately avoiding looking at me while she waited for my answer.

"Why? Do you want to be my sponsor? Keep me on the straight and narrow?"

Her eyes met mine. "If that's what it takes."

"I wasn't planning on going out, no." I hadn't done that lately, and I intended to try to keep that record going. Actually, I hadn't done that in a while, despite what I let McKenna believe.

"That's really good, Knox."

Time for a new topic. I wasn't okay sitting here with a beautiful girl calming discussing my last fuck.

I cleared my throat. "So, what's your story? Don't you have someplace you need to be?"

She flinched at my words.

Shit.

"That's not what I meant," I said quickly. "I'm sorry."

She shrugged, then looked away. "I heard what you said to your brothers. That I'm just your counselor. I'm sorry I keep showing up here."

"You are my counselor, but I shouldn't have said that."

She looked down, her confidence fading at my admission. Using two fingers, I lifted her chin. Her gaze slid intimately from my eyes to my mouth, and a warm feeling burned in my chest.

"What's that look for?" I asked, my voice coming out too thick. Her gaze slipped away from mine until once again my fingers under her chin reminded her not to hide from me. "You're beautiful," I whispered.

"Knox," she murmured, her voice a tiny plea. "I wish we'd met under different circumstances. My being your addiction counselor complicates things."

"Why can't I just be a man, and you just be a woman?"

"You're in recovery. I can't be a temptation to you."

I swallowed heavily. Too late for that. My balls were aching with the need to sink inside her.

"We all have certain wants and desires, McKenna. It doesn't make them wrong. We're only human."

Indecision flashed in her eyes and her gaze zeroed in on my mouth. If I had to guess, I'd say she was thinking about what it would be like to kiss me. It seemed that good-girl McKenna had a naughty side to her. Every ounce of her wanted that kiss. I could read it all over her, from her flushed chest to the thrumming pulse in her neck. I'd be willing to bet it had been a long time since a man touched her. Her body's responses were too obvious, and I could read the want and curiosity all over her.

I leaned forward just slightly, wetting my lips. She swallowed, her eyes tracking the movements. Angling my head to hers, I paused, stopping myself. Why? To prove a point. We were mammals, we reacted to the opposite sex. It was biology. We were born to breed, to reproduce. Men especially—to spread around our seed. Just the fact that I stopped myself proved that I didn't have a problem. Only I wasn't sure if I was trying to convince McKenna or myself.

She pulled back, just the slightest bit. "This can't happen, Knox."

"Then let me go about things the correct way then.

Let me take you out. A proper date." As soon as I'd blurted it, I had no idea where that came from.

"I can't," she whispered, looking down at her hands in her lap.

"Can't or don't want to?"

"Isn't it the same thing?" She looked up and studied me with wide blue eyes.

"No. *Can't* means you won't jeopardize our professional relationship in group, and *don't want to* means you'd be lying by saying you don't feel this pull between us."

McKenna looked down and sighed. "Knox, don't do this."

"I won't push you. Not tonight. But we will talk about this."

"I should go," she murmured.

"Yeah, me too." I blew out a heavy sigh.

"You're leaving?" she asked, her voice wavering.

I shrugged.

"Where are you going?" McKenna rose to her feet, concern etching a line between her brows.

"Out," I said sharply.

"Don't do something you'll regret." She stepped closer and placed her warm palm against my chest.

She could probably feel the steady knock of my heartbeat, the indecision in my posture. But none of that mattered. I couldn't put myself in a position to get too close to McKenna. I wouldn't trick her into thinking I was somebody I wasn't. This was me. Rough around the edges and enough baggage to take down an airliner.

"Let me go, McKenna." I shrugged away from her touch.

"You know what, Knox?" she bit out, turning to face me. "Don't bother coming to group this week."

She left a few moments later and I was too wound up to even offer to drive her home. I felt rejected and angry. I wanted to put my fist through the wall. Instead, I checked to be sure all three boys were safe in their rooms, then shoved on my boots, grabbed my keys and a handful of condoms, and was out the door.

I'd pushed McKenna the slightest bit—just to test the waters—and she'd done exactly what I'd known she'd do. She ran. Left me with a pounding heart and a hot anger burning inside me that needed to be squelched. She might have been good at acting like she cared, but that was all it was. Some do-gooder act to soothe her conscience for whatever it was she'd done to deserve to counsel dickheads like me for a living.

Although I hadn't been here in weeks, I soon found myself pulling into the parking lot of the strip club, the neon signs bathing the dark interior of my Jeep in light, like a beacon pulling me forward.

I'd put myself out there, tried to go about things the legitimate way, and it had gotten me nowhere. McKenna was different, and I knew I had to do things her way if I wanted to be close to her. I was definitely willing to try.

But she'd turned me down without a second thought. It was always the same thing. Opening yourself up ended in rejection. Period. And tonight I needed a sure thing. The tension inside me evoked by being so near a beautiful woman and unable to do a damn thing about it had left me unsatisfied. I needed relief. At the same time, I knew that in the morning, whatever relief I felt would be marked with regret. But it was too late to turn back.

I entered the club and sank into the shadows, letting the bass-filled music drown out my own thoughts and reservations.

Chapter Eleven

Realizing Knox was going out, that he was choosing his addiction over me, caused a stabbing sensation to pierce my chest. All I wanted was the safety and comfort of my own bed right now.

I'd thought we were making progress. He'd invited me in for pizza, included me in their little celebration. The way he'd looked at me tonight when we were all alone told me he did feel something for me. But then just as quickly, his eyes had gone blank and he pulled back, closing himself off once again.

When I arrived home, I shoved my key in the lock and pushed open the door.

Brian rose from the couch, turning to face me, his expression pinched and angry. "Where the hell have you been? I called your cell six times."

Oops. I'd left my phone at the bottom of my purse all evening. There was no one I'd wanted to talk to when I was with the Bauer brothers. I smiled, remembering the way Tucker had curled himself against my side and Luke had opened up. Tonight had felt like something special. A tiny connection that I hadn't felt in a long time.

Knowing I was terrible at lying, I took a deep breath, dropped my purse on the counter, and turned to face Brian. "I was over at Knox's, having dinner."

His eyes widened and his jaw dropped open. "Are you insane? You went to that—that animal's house? Alone?" I'd made the mistake of mentioning Knox's name after Brian had seen me talking to him after group. "Do you have any idea what could have happened—what does happen to girls like you? Watch the evening news more often, because that was stupid and reckless."

"Girls like me?" My hand went defensively to my hip.

"Yes, girls like you—young, attractive, and sweet. What were you thinking, McKenna? Oh, let me guess, you thought you could get through to him, put him back together?" He huffed out an exasperated breath, like my helping someone was the most absurd thing he'd ever heard. I wanted to point out that I had a degree in counseling, but knew that wouldn't help my cause.

"We weren't alone. He lives with his brothers."

"Oh, that makes me feel so much better." His voice dripped in sarcasm.

"You're overreacting, Brian. Everything was fine." *Was.* Until the end when something in him snapped and he all but kicked me out.

"God, you're naive. I know you're trying to save the world and fix everyone and everything around you, but this is taking it too far. I've tolerated your running all over the city, playing Miss Martyr, but this isn't healthy and you know it."

He's tolerated it? My heartbeat kicked up in my chest, my blood pressure jumping up. He didn't have any right to act this way.

"You could have been hurt," he said, softer this time.

"Yeah, well I wasn't." Not physically, anyway. "Stop acting like an overprotective older brother, Brian. Everything's under control." I pushed past him on my way to my room.

"That's all you see me as, isn't it?" he asked, his voice dropping an octave lower.

Rather than begin a conversation I so didn't want to have, I closed my bedroom door and mumbled a good-night in his direction. I was supposed to be getting my life together. Taking this job, moving to the city, all of it was supposed to be my fresh start. My do-over. Instead I felt more confused and alone than ever.

I regretted how I'd handled things with Knox tonight. I drove him away, told him not to come back to group. My feelings were too tangled up to properly be his counselor. I knew I was treating him different from anyone else. For all I knew, they could all be carrying on relations outside of class. I was holding him to a higher standard because I liked him. And I wanted him to like me back.

God, I was pathetic.

I had to force myself out of bed in the morning. Some days were tougher than others, and after last night, I wasn't feeling particularly put together and ready to face the day.

I didn't know why the sadness hit me harder some days. Maybe it was PMS. Maybe it was the sting of Knox's rejection, but I sat up in bed, my legs folded underneath me, fighting back tears and wishing I could talk to my mom. Knowing my parents no longer existed in this world was too much to process. The weight of their deaths crashed down on me and made it difficult to breathe. I felt like a massive dinosaur was sitting on my chest. A feeling that everyone told me should have faded by now, but was alive and present. I just needed to keep busy to block out the pain. It helped me carry on when I no longer wanted to.

That was what I focused on as I laced up my tennis shoes and threw my hair into a ponytail. I was meeting Belinda for coffee this morning to discuss the progress of my group, and then I was headed to a shelter to volunteer. I couldn't keep running off to see Knox. He wasn't someone to rely on. He was sick and needed help, and I would help him the best I could. I had only myself to rely on. Which was why I'd signed up to be part of a cleaning crew, wiping down cots and mattresses, scrubbing toilets, and mopping floors at the shelter today. If that didn't distract me from thoughts of Knox and this dangerous game I was playing with him, nothing would.

When I arrived at Cup O' Brew, I found Belinda already seated in a comfy armchair at the back of the café. I waved to her, and then ordered a hot chocolate at the counter. I even splurged and got whipped cream, hoping the extra sugar would help elevate my mood.

My insides were burning with curiosity, wondering if Knox had gone out looking for a girl after I'd left. Of course he had. Why wouldn't he? And I shouldn't feel the things I did. It would have been normal to be worried about his safety, his health, his mental wellness. Instead I felt a combination of jealousy and regret. Maybe if I'd stayed and talked to him, he'd have chosen me instead of the path he went down. It was all I'd thought about since last night, and I had the dark circles under my eyes to prove it.

Carrying my paper cup, I crossed the room to meet Belinda.

"You look well." She rose and gave me a brief hug.

I was good at hiding how miserable and alone I felt. And at knowing how to apply under-eye concealer to cover up the fact I'd spent the night tossing and turning.

"Thanks. You do too. I love your scarf."

The truth was Belinda went completely overboard with accessories. Bright pink hoop earrings, a rabbit brooch on her sweater, a colorful scarf wrapped around her neck, and a giant purple handbag. It was enough color to give me a headache. I slid into the wide leather armchair across from her and took a sip of my hot chocolate.

129

"Tell me how it's going leading the new group."

I fidgeted with my cup, like Belinda would somehow read my thoughts and know all I thought about these days was Knox. "It's going well. I have about twelve regular members and occasionally get drop-ins too." I wasn't quite sure what she wanted to hear. Did she want updates on each individual and their progress?

"Good. And how about participation?"

"Participation in class is average. Some talk more than others, those who are quiet pay attention thought and often nod along." *Except Knox; he only shares when we're alone together.*

Belinda took a notebook from her giant purse and flipped it open to scribble something down. "And engagement with fellow group members? How's that?"

"Engagement?" I had no idea what she meant.

"Do they support each other, do they mingle after group is over and talk? Exchange phone numbers? Things like that."

"Oh. Um, no, not really." Most people fled the room as soon as the hour was up, like they were desperate to get away.

130

"It's something I'd like you to encourage. This is their group. They are there to support each other. It's your job to connect them, encourage them to build friendships inside the group."

I looked at Belinda, wondering how I'd accomplish that. My mind flashed to Knox again and I imagined partnering him up with Bill or Donald for sharing time, and knew that wouldn't work. But why was I even thinking of that when I'd told Knox not to bother coming back? Feelings of overwhelming guilt pierced through me, and I struggled to remain composed.

Belinda leaned forward in her chair. "We can provide the structure of a one-hour weekly meeting, but for most people that's not enough. They need a support system of others who care about their progress and success. It also teaches them there is a way to get their social needs met through healthy interactions, rather than just with sex."

She was talking about friendship, and suddenly I realized that I was that person for Knox. Before I ruined things, he was slowly starting to open up. I had hoped over time it would lead to his recovery, though it wasn't my motivator for spending time with him. The truth was, I liked him. I liked being near him. I didn't think Belinda would approve of that, though. Just the thought of telling her I'd been to his house, spent time alone with him, made my chest flush. No, I would need to keep that to myself.

"I'll work on it," I promised.

"Good. We'll meet again in a few weeks, and I want to hear about your progress and who you've connected in the group."

I made a move to get up, but Belinda held up a hand to stop me.

"There's one more thing. I'm sending a young woman to your group. Amanda's a little different from our usual case. I've been individually counseling her, but I think she could benefit from a group setting. She has a sex and love addiction. She looks for Mr. Right in all the wrong places. She even tried to trap her last hookup into a relationship by getting pregnant. It obviously didn't work out the way she wanted—she's now pregnant and alone and has come forward for help."

"How far along is she?"

"Three months. She's not showing yet, but I wanted you to know her background. She's about your age, so I thought perhaps you two might connect. Tread lightly with this one. She's fragile."

Join the club. Maybe I wasn't in any position to be giving out counseling advice with the state of my own life, but I nodded. "I will. And thanks for believing in me." Her faith in me made me feel even guiltier about my growing feelings for Knox.

But I needed to put that out of my mind. I was due at the shelter and had a day of hard work ahead of me.

Chapter Twelve

As I lay in bed tossing and turning, I worked over and over again in my mind what had happened between me and McKenna. I shouldn't want her. I wasn't the right man for her. She should be with someone educated, polite, and well-mannered. Not some asshole like me who had experienced enough loss to turn my heart into a hollow drum.

I knew one thing for sure—I wasn't good enough for her. And I'd been stupid to even fantasize that I might be. Last night had cemented the deal; she'd run and I had too. Straight into the arms of a stripper. Temporary bliss was all I had these days. Finding a willing, wet girl to sink into provided twenty minutes of mind-numbing sensation, and I couldn't give that up. Going out a couple of nights a week was my distraction. And thoughts of McKenna were starting to interfere with that. She was dangerous. I'd turned off my emotions a long time ago as my only source of protection, and I couldn't have her tearing those walls down.

But morning light brought a fresh perspective to everything and I wanted her. Why deny myself?

Tracking her down was harder than I thought it would be. Her asshole of a roommate hadn't wanted to help me; that was crystal clear. He looked at me through squinted eyes, presumably guessing that all I wanted was to get inside her panties. And while that might have been true, today I actually just wanted to apologize.

She'd taken a chance coming over last night, groceries in hand, offering to cook for us. I couldn't remember the last time someone had done anything like that for us. Not since my mother. And when I realized that I couldn't get what I wanted—her—I'd gone all macho caveman, running her out and heading to my old stomping grounds.

Little good it had done me. I'd sat there sulking like a pussy, unable to stop thinking about her, until I'd finally just gone home and crawled into bed alone.

But after I applied some pressure this morning, Brian had finally told me that she was volunteering at a shelter today, and said good luck finding her. It turned out the city of Chicago had dozens of shelters. I'd visited six of them already and was almost about to call off my mission when lucky number seven turned out to be the right one.

Letting myself inside the front doors, I was struck with the stench of sweat and mildew. I approached a woman seated behind what appeared to be bulletproof glass. This was the place McKenna came in her free time?

"Can I help you?" she asked.

"Yeah, I'm looking for a girl named McKenna. Is she here today?"

"I'm sorry, I can't tell you that." She crossed her arms over her chest.

I thought about describing her to the woman, but realized there'd be no way I could do that without sounding like a prick. *She's the perfect height to fit against me, curves that would bring a man to his knees, an ass you just want to admire, and tits to fit perfectly in the palm of your hand.*

So I lied. "I'm here to volunteer with my friend McKenna, but I'm not sure which shelter she's at today."

"Oh. You're here to volunteer? Well, come on then. I'll take you to her." The woman rose to her feet and motioned for me to follow her to a door just down the hall. Seconds later, it opened and I followed her inside. She led me through a series of hallways, and we passed by a large commercial kitchen and several bathrooms before finally entering a huge room filled with stacks and stacks of cots.

McKenna was sitting on the floor in the middle of the room, a bucket of soapy water at her side, wiping down a cot with a sponge. The woman turned and left me there at the entrance to the room, just staring at McKenna. I was too taken aback to say anything just yet. Who was this beautiful girl who gave so selflessly, who worked tirelessly to serve others?

As I watched her scrubbing down the cot, I was struck with the realization that McKenna was a good person, a rare find these days. She looked so tiny and out of place in this dirty, windowless room on her hands and knees cleaning up other people's filth. Her hair was tied up in a hasty knot and her cheeks were rosy and pink from exertion. She looked like a blue-eyed, shimmering-haired angel in these grim surroundings.

"Need a hand?" I called out, stepping forward to enter the room.

"Knox?" She rose to her feet. "What are you doing here?"

"I came to help out today. Brian told me where to

137

find you."

"You talked to Brian?"

I nodded, not bothering to mention that he hadn't wanted to help me, or that he'd been a complete asshole. Uneasy, I stood before her and surveyed our surroundings. "So, where do you need me?"

"Why are you here?"

"I'm sorry for last night; I was an ass." I stayed quiet while she looked me over. She was waiting for me to say more, so I took a step closer. "I'm not good at apologies and heartfelt displays, but I truly did come here today to help out. If you want me."

She chewed on her lip in indecision and for a second I thought she was going to push me away. "Okay," she said.

"Okay?"

She nodded, smiling at me. "I'm glad you're here. And I'm sorry about what I said last night. Of course I want you back in group."

"Don't worry. I knew you were bluffing about that." I rubbed my hands together. "So, what's our task?"

138

"See all those cots?" She pointed to several six-foot-high stacks of cots lining the far wall. "We need to wash all of them."

"All of them?" There had to be hundreds. "And you were going to do that all by yourself?"

She nodded. Shit, that would have taken her all day. Didn't she have anything better to do with her time than sit in a dank room cleaning for hours on end for no pay and little recognition?

I couldn't really picture her prioritizing going shopping at the mall or getting her nails done above this type of work, though. This was just who she was. I'd spent very little time with her, and I already knew that. She was a giver. Would she be as giving and accommodating in the bedroom? A pang of lust jabbed at my gut at the thought. *Down, boy.*

"I'll get you a bucket of soapy water and a sponge," she said, heading to the exit. I couldn't help but watch the sway of her ass encased in tight denim. She really was beautiful. Even in her jeans and T-shirt.

When she returned, I was unstacking the cots and lining them up in rows so we could wash each one. The thought of McKenna doing all this manual labor alone made me glad I came. This was a big job for one person.

McKenna returned, setting the bucket down beside me and splashing me with warm soapy water in the process. I considered engaging her in a water fight, but decided against it. She took this work seriously and I would show her that I could too.

We worked side by side for the better part of an hour, making only a small dent in the work ahead of us. I wondered if McKenna was set on getting through the entire bunch, or if I could talk her into going out to lunch. Looking over at her, I knew there was no way she was leaving until the job was done. She worked without pause or complaint as determination blazed in her eyes.

Dropping my sponge into the bucket of water, I went to unstack another set of cots for us to wash, moving the damp ones to the far side of the room where they could air dry while McKenna went to dump out our buckets of dirty water and refill them. My fingers were already pruned and my back was aching from sitting hunched over on the floor. But I wouldn't complain. Not while McKenna was still working so adamantly to clean these beds for people she didn't even know, would never meet. I had no idea why this was so important to her, but I could tell that it was.

We fell into a routine, my moving and unstacking cots, McKenna refilling our water, and each of us washing in silence. Seven hours later and finally we were down to the last couple of cots.

"Oh, Christ." I swore, pushing the filthy cot away from me. Someone had deliberately buried this one at the bottom of the stack.

"What's wrong?" She peered over at me from across the room.

There was shit smeared on the cot in front of me. If she really expected me to wipe up someone else's crap, she was crazy. "This one needs to be taken out back and burned."

"What?" She laughed, rising to her feet and crossing the room to stand over me. "Oh." She frowned, looking down at the brown stains.

"Someone shit the bed," I joked dryly.

"Just scrub it off."

"Hell no."

"You change Bailee's diapers. What's the difference?"

141

I cocked an eyebrow at her. "She's a baby. Babies shit their pants, this is different. This is probably from a grown-ass man. That's a whole different ball game."

"Fine, I'll do this one." She dropped to her knees to kneel beside me.

"No way I'm letting you do that. We seriously can't just throw this one away? Surely they have a dumpster out back."

"Knox, we're not throwing away the poop cot. It'll come clean. They're short on cots as it is."

Fuck me, the things I'd do for this girl. I soaked the sponge in soapy water and began scrubbing at the cot, fighting back the gagging in my throat.

When I was done, she giggled and said, "That wasn't so bad, was it?"

"I need a shower."

"They have showers here."

I rolled my eyes. The idea of showering here made me feel even dirtier somehow. "Come on. We're going out."

"We are? I was going to find the director and see if I

could help with anything else."

"McKenna, we've been here all day. My hands are pruned, my knees are sore from kneeling on a concrete floor, and I was just subjected to human feces. We're leaving."

She giggled again. "Okay, I suppose you're right. We did enough for one day."

I was about to correct her and let her know I'd done enough for a lifetime, but I didn't want her to change her mind about leaving, so I shut my mouth and trailed behind her.

After a stop in the restroom, where I doused my hands, forearms, and even my face and neck in scalding hot soapy water, I waited in the hallway for McKenna in the hallway. While she washed up, I called home to check on my brothers and let them know I wouldn't be home for a while. When she emerged, McKenna had secured her hair in a neat braid hanging over her shoulder. How she could look pretty after the day we'd had, I had no idea.

Her eyes met mine and she tipped her head shyly. I needed to be careful about how I looked at her. I was watching her like I wanted to eat her alive. Hell, I wasn't opposed to it.

"Where are we going?" she asked as I led her out into the fading sunlight.

Chapter Thirteen

I held open the door for McKenna and we entered the small diner just blocks from the shelter. It was already after four, and after skipping breakfast and lunch, I was starving. Of course when I'd set out this morning to find McKenna, I hadn't known I was signing up for an all-day volunteer activity.

I asked the hostess for a table for two and noticed her gaze flicker between me and McKenna. Did she think we were here on a date? Shit, were we on a date? I never did things like this—take a girl out to eat. Even if it was just to a crappy diner. I hadn't done anything like this in years. Mostly because of the boys. I felt only mildly guilty about not being home when they got home from school. Something told me they'd approve of my being with McKenna, though.

McKenna surprised me by asking for a box of crayons at the hostess station. Then we slid into a squeaky leather booth and McKenna accepted her menu, smiling at me.

"What?" I asked.

"Thanks for helping today." She flipped over her place mat and began doodling on the back in purple crayon. The girl continued to surprise me.

I sensed that something between us had changed today. I'd shown her a different side of myself and put us on more equal footing. It wasn't what I had planned for my one day off from work this week, but I was glad I'd stayed and helped her. I couldn't imagine her doing all that alone today; she'd still be there. I knew people gave their time and resources to causes that were important to them, and I'll admit, it had felt good to give back today, but either McKenna had the soul of a saint, or her need to serve was something different.

"What drives you to volunteer, McKenna?"

Looking up from coloring, she chewed on her lower lip. "It's just what I do. I spend pretty much every free minute at the homeless shelter."

"You do this to avoid being at home?" If that dickhead Brian was making her uncomfortable, I'd head right over there and handle it.

"Not exactly. More like to fill my time. I don't like being alone with too much time to think. It's just…not good for me."

I wondered what worries could possibly be weighing on her mind. "What are you running from?"

She went back to coloring and I realized I didn't know much about this beautiful girl who sat in front of me. She grabbed the brown crayon and drew a two-story house, coloring in the windows with blue curtains, and then drew three stick figures in front of the house. On one of them she colored long dark brown hair and blue eyes, and I realized she was drawing me something from her childhood.

I watched her in silence, wondering if she was trying to give me a clue about her life. The thought of someone harming her rose the hairs on the back of my neck. Before she finished her drawing, the waitress delivered our orders—a salad and soup for her, and a burger for me. Setting her drawing aside for the moment, we dug into the food in silence, the weight of our conversation still hanging over us.

McKenna picked at her salad, using the tines of her fork to push a cherry tomato around the plate.

147

"What's on your mind?" I asked, wiping my mouth on the napkin.

Pretty blue eyes pierced mine as she hesitated to answer.

"Say it, angel."

"When I met you...I don't know. I could feel your pain and knew you'd experienced more than your fair share of trauma too. I felt connected to you."

I knew what she meant, but that didn't mean I wanted to encourage her attachment to me. I would only end up hurting and disappointing her. Even if I did everything in my power not to, that was my track record with women.

I pushed my plate away, my appetite all but vanishing. "McKenna, I'm not going to deny that we have a connection. We do."

"But?" she supplied, a trace of sarcasm in her voice.

"But...I fuck random girls. I use them for sex. I'm not a good guy. You shouldn't be so nice to me."

"You've made bad choices. You've messed up. But you're not a bad guy. I see the way you are with your brothers, and attending group, that's your way of trying to

148

get better. You're not going to scare me off so easily, Knox."

My participation in her little meetings was practically court-mandated, and honestly, the only reason I'd continued going was because of my attraction to her. The waitress appeared again, this time to collect our half-eaten meals.

"Will you tell me more about how this all started," she asked.

"What do you want to know?"

She shrugged, looking down at the vinyl-covered table. "Whatever you want to share."

McKenna passed me the box of crayons and I chuckled, flipping over my own place mat to the blank white side. "Is this some type of counseling technique, drawing out your feelings?"

"No." She laughed, her tone light. "I just like to color."

I plucked a crayon from the box, noticing it was pink. But I wouldn't complain about the choice in color. If this was what she wanted, I would try to get in touch with my softer side. I wasn't ready to tell her everything, but after the day we'd shared—scrubbing shit off cots—I felt more open with her than anyone else.

"When my dad left, everything fell on me. I got a part-time job and took care of the boys. It would have been easier to drop out of school and get a full-time job, but I was set on finishing up my senior year. I knew I needed to graduate or I'd never be able to really provide for them."

I scribbled something on the paper in front of me, not really paying attention to what I was drawing. "All week I went to school, worked, put food on the table, and at night, I made sure homework got done, supervised bath time, enforced rules and curfews. And I had to put up with strange looks at parent-teacher conferences and doctors' appointments. Eventually I applied for legal guardianship."

McKenna's eyes stayed downcast on her own page, which made opening up easier somehow. She passed me another crayon, green this time, and I continued drawing – little crooked designs that made no sense but seemed to calm me.

"By the time Saturday night rolled around, I'd wait until the boys were in bed and I'd go down the road to the corner bar, where they never carded, and grab a few beers to relax. Then I'd find a pretty girl to sink into to forget my troubles." There was more, but I wasn't ready to talk about it.

McKenna sucked in a deep breath, temporarily pausing in her drawing.

I wouldn't sugarcoat this. If she wanted in, I would let her see the true me, faults and all.

"I did what was expected of me. I take care of my brothers, pay the bills, follow up on homework. But at night, after everyone goes to bed, the emptiness and loneliness become too much. I need relief and that's how I seek it."

I couldn't believe he was telling me all this. In group, he was all penetrating gazes and silent intensity. But one-on-one, he was making himself vulnerable to me. I was straddling the line between being me—a regular girl who was interested in a guy, and a counselor who wanted to help him heal. I had no idea which one of us would win out.

Knox slapped a few bills down on the table, enough to cover both our meals.

"I can pay for myself." I reached inside my purse for my wallet.

"Next time."

I didn't know if there would be a next time, but I nodded. "Okay."

"Should we go?"

"Sure." I rose from the booth and stretched, my back straightening reluctantly. I smiled, realizing I would sleep well tonight from the day's manual labor.

I figured Knox was going to drive me straight home after we ate, but he surprised me by asking if I would go somewhere with him. I blindly agreed without knowing our destination. When he pulled to a stop in front of a deserted playground, I waited, unsure of what we were doing here.

"Come on. This place has the best slide in the world."

I watched in fascination as he climbed from the Jeep and headed toward the playground. I'd never seen him in a mood so playful and carefree. He was captivating.

"Knox! Wait up," I called, jogging behind him. He sat down on a swing and I joined him, each of us toeing the gravel to gain momentum.

He looked lost in his thoughts, and though there were a million questions I wanted to ask him, I waited, letting him enjoy the quiet moment he seemed to be having. We swung side by side, looking out at the park.

"I haven't been here in almost twenty years," he said finally. "I must have been about three when my mother worked in this part of town. She used to drop me off at this Russian lady's house while she went to work. Sometimes after work when she picked me up, we'd come here before going home."

153

I realized with Jaxon being four years younger, Knox would have been an only child at that time. It was sweet that he had memories of just him and his mom. I wondered if thinking of her made him sad, like it did for me. We sat in silence, swinging until the sky was growing pink with the impending sunset.

"So is that the famous slide?" I asked, tipping my head toward the monstrosity.

There didn't appear to be anything special about it. It was an old rusted-out metal slide, but I could tell in Knox's mind, it was somewhere sacred he'd built fond memories with his mom. And I wouldn't question it. I had my own version of this slide built up in my mind too.

"That's her." He smiled.

"Well, I've gotta try this out." I hopped off my swing in the middle of its upward arc and ventured toward the rusty contraption. "Are you sure this thing is safe?" I climbed up the bottom rung of the ladder and stopped, testing my weight.

He shrugged. "Should be fine as long as you're up-to-date on your tetanus shot."

Scampering up the ladder before I chickened out, I

plopped my butt down so I was perched at the top, my legs stretched out in front of me. Knox positioned himself below me at the bottom of the slide, and grinned up at me playfully.

"Come on down, I'll catch you."

I pushed myself forward, expecting to slide down easily. Instead, my jeans rubbed against the dull metal and I scooted about two inches. We both cracked up laughing. "That was anticlimactic." With gravity proving to be no help, I used my feet to pull my pull myself down, scurrying the entire length of the slide until I came to an unsatisfying stop in front of Knox.

"It was better when I was three." He extended a hand and I accepted, letting him pull me to my feet.

"Such a letdown," I joked, nudging my shoulder with his.

"Hmm." His eyes lazily traveled over me. "I'll make it up to you."

"Oh yeah? How?"

He pointed across the street from the park. "See that coffee shop?" I nodded, and he said, "I'll buy you a hot chocolate."

155

"Deal."

While we sipped hot cocoa at a little café table, Knox called home once again to check on the boys. I loved how dedicated he was to them. It almost made me feel a little guilty for hogging him all day. But there was no denying I'd enjoyed today immensely.

"I have something to tell you," he said.

"What is it?" I waited, breathless. Anytime Knox let me in was a small win.

"My test results came today."

"And? Did you open them?"

He nodded, smiling crookedly. "I'm clean."

Wow. "That's amazing news." A contented little sigh escaped my lips.

"I'm glad you made me do it."

It was the little moments like this that made my job so rewarding. Knox wouldn't have gone on his own, and I was happy that I was the one to encourage him. I was even happier at the results.

I drank my hot chocolate slowly, savoring it, almost like I was afraid to take the last sip because it meant our day together would be over. As it neared time to leave, both of us grew quiet as the easy mood from earlier all but evaporated. I remembered what Knox said about the night, and I prayed he wasn't planning on going out to one of his usual haunts to pick up a woman. That thought crushed me.

"You okay?" he asked, setting down his own cup as if he sensed my somber mood.

"Fine," I lied.

"I should take you home." He might have voiced the words, but his body language wasn't on board. He was leaning toward me, his elbows on the table and his gaze piercing mine.

"Okay," I breathed. It was dark outside, nearly eight at night. Logic told me I should probably go home, even if the rest of me didn't want to.

As we neared my apartment, a feeling of sadness settled over me. It had been a magical day. I'd expected to work at the shelter all day and then go home to have dinner with Brian. *Oops*. I'd forgotten all about dinner with Bri. I'd just tell him my work at the shelter ran late. Never mind this glow to my cheeks and lightheartedness from spending the day with Knox.

Rather than just dropping me off at the curb, Knox switched the ignition off and walked me to the door. We stood together under the little yellow porch light, watching each other. I couldn't help glancing at his full lips and wondering if they'd taste like chocolate.

Knox shoved his hands into his pockets. He was stalling. Neither of us was ready to say good night.

"McKenna, I—"

Before Knox could finish whatever it was he was going to say, the door flew open and Brian stood between us, fuming. His eyes flashed from me to Knox and back again. Something told me he wasn't pissed that I'd missed dinner; it was finding me here with Knox that had him on edge.

I shoved past them into the foyer of the apartment. "Geez, Bri, relax. I'm sorry I missed dinner." I tossed my purse onto the counter and felt a pang of guilt seeing the plate of food he'd prepared and covered in plastic wrap for me.

"Where have you been?" Brian shouted, coming in behind me.

Knox bit out a curse, his posture stiffening as he

stepped in front of me protectively. "She was with me. What's the problem?"

"The problem?" Brian crossed the room to stand directly in front of Knox. He was a fraction shorter and with much less definition in his arms and chest, but you wouldn't know it by the way he was puffing his chest out, acting like a caged gorilla. "The problem is that I know what you are. I saw you at that meeting."

"What I am? And what's that?" Knox asked, casually taking a step closer.

"Not good enough for her." Brian tipped his head toward me.

"And someone like you is? Why don't you let McKenna decide that for herself?"

"I've been protecting this girl from cocky assholes like you for years, and I'm not about to stop now."

"Brian!" I hissed through clenched teeth. I wouldn't have him insulting Knox.

Knox dropped his head back, looking up at the ceiling, and let out a short bark of laughter. "You want her for yourself."

Brian lunged at Knox, pushing both hands against his

chest in a hard shove. Knox staggered two steps back into our living room.

"Be sure you want this." Knox's hands curled into fists at his sides, and my insides twisted violently. "McKenna?" Knox's narrowed eyes found mine. "Go to your room."

No way was I going in my room just then. They weren't actually going to fight over me, were they?

Brian rushed forward again and Knox sidestepped him, instinctively drawing him farther away from where I stood rooted in place, my jaw hanging open. Brian wasn't violent; he wasn't a fighter. Not even in high school when most boys had raging teenage hormones, he was calm and in control. But I'd also never seen that vein throbbing in his forehead.

"You know why she's with you, don't you?" Brian taunted. "She's a fixer. Always has been. Adopting stray dogs from the shelter, stopping to help wildlife cross the road, befriending the new kids at school…that's all this is. You're a problem"—he poked a provoking finger into Knox's chest—"that she wants to fix."

Knox's gaze flashed to mine and Brian took that split-second distraction to haul back and land a punch in the center of Knox's cheek.

I winced as the contact threw Knox's head back.

Not wasting a second, Knox rushed Brian, knocking him to the floor and landing several punishing hits to his face and body.

"Stop! You guys, stop it!" I clawed desperately at Knox's shoulders, trying to dislodge him from where he held Brian captive. Brian landed a quick hit to Knox's nose, sending blood pouring from both nostrils. Frightened, I cowered on the floor, scrambling backward on hands and knees as big soggy tears rolled down my cheeks.

Both men caught their breath, their fight seemingly over. Knox's eyes met mine and I read his expression as clear as if he'd voiced the words. *I'm sorry.*

His shoulders down and his gaze fixed on the floor, Knox left, closing the door quietly behind him. There was something about the way he'd shut the door that stuck with me. Had he slammed it closed, I would have felt better. I would understand his anger. He was just attacked verbally and physically in my apartment by my roommate. His careful exit felt like defeat. Not a physical defeat—he could have taken Brian—I saw that in the power of his punches when he had Brian pinned down. No, it was more like he knew he'd lost me before we'd even started anything, and he was quietly walking away and letting Brian win.

The thought didn't sit well with me. I wanted him to fight for me, to pull me from this corner and wipe my tears, tell me that no one and nothing would keep us apart. But he hadn't. It was all a twisted little fantasy. Knox didn't feel for me the way I did for him.

I remembered the way blood had erupted from his nose, and wondered if he was okay to drive home. Sheesh, I hadn't even offered to help him, given him a tissue, apologized for the brutal way my roommate had behaved. Knox had been nothing but a gentleman all day, and he deserved none of what Brian delivered.

"McKenna." Brian stood over me, hands on his hips. "I know you want me to apologize—"

"Save it, Brian." I leaped to my feet and grabbed my purse from the counter, slamming the apartment door behind me.

When I arrived at Knox's place, all was quiet and

dark. The front door was unlocked and I let myself in, not wanting to wake anyone who might be asleep. A lamp glowed softly next to the couch, but no one was around, on the first floor at least. I crept up the creaking staircase, my fingers grazing the wooden banister as I headed to the attic.

It was dark and silent on the third floor too, and I wondered if Knox was asleep. It had been almost an hour since he'd left my apartment, thanks to the city bus schedule, and it was entirely possible he was already asleep in bed. The thought of finding him, shirtless and stretched out on the mattress, sent a little thrill through me. I promised myself I wouldn't ogle him. Okay, maybe just for a second I'd allow myself to appreciate the view. Then I'd wake him and check on his injuries. See if he needed anything and apologize for my psycho roommate.

Tiptoeing across the creaky wooden floor, I felt like an intruder. I'd probably scare him half to death. "Knox," I whispered loudly. "It's me." The room was so dark, I couldn't even tell if there was movement from under the covers. "Knox?" I flipped on the lamp beside the small couch for light. Glancing up, I realized his bed was empty. Knox wasn't here.

Realization struck like a whack to the side of the head. He'd gone out. After spending all day bonding with me, showing me a sweet side to him by working at the shelter, he'd still chosen to go out. I didn't want to jump to conclusions, but really, what other possibilities were there? It was late and his brothers were asleep. He'd told me himself, this was how he operated. I just thought I'd be the one to get through to him, and it stung knowing that my efforts hadn't made one bit of difference.

I sat down on his bed, hating myself for how betrayed I felt. It wasn't fair to Knox. He was in treatment. He was bound to mess up now and then, and tonight with Brian had probably been a trigger for him. I knew he didn't handle stress well—that he turned straight to sex. What had I really expected when he left my apartment looking broken and defeated?

And it had nothing to do with being outmatched by Brian. I'd seen the restraint Knox displayed, the tension in his shoulders as he held himself back from doing any real damage. He'd spared Brian, and the only reason could have possibly been because of me. Because of my friendship with Bri.

I remained on Knox's bed waiting for him. I would

wait all night if I had to; I needed to make things right between us. When my eyes grew droopy, I lay down, curling on my side against his pillow.

The sounds of running water and rustling coming from the hallway woke me. I crawled from bed, groggy and wondering what time it was. Since I was pretty sure only Knox used the bathroom on the third floor, I tapped my knuckles against the door. "Knox?"

"Not now, McKenna," Knox grumbled from inside.

No way was I letting him patch up Brian's handiwork alone. "I'm coming in." I pushed the door open and entered the tiny steam-filled bathroom. Blinking through the vapors, I found him slumped on the floor, his head hanging in his hands.

He stared up at me with unfocused eyes. "What are you doing here?" he slurred.

"Have you been drinking?"

He chuckled. "No, officer."

"Knox, this isn't funny. You're wasted. Did you drive home like this?"

"Relax. People get drunk, and no, I walked home."

"Where did you go?" I assumed it was somewhere local, since he'd walked home, but I was too afraid to ask my real question—*What did you do?*

"I went out. Had a few drinks." He shrugged.

"And?" I probed. I had to know; even if it crushed me.

"And I picked up a girl, and I couldn't even fuck her. Is that what you wanted to hear?"

My breath stuttered.

He pushed his hands into his hair, tangling it in disarray. "Your sad blue eyes wouldn't leave my brain. I couldn't stop comparing your subtle feminine scent to her harsh perfume. Your touchable soft waves to her too-stiff curls." Looking up to meet my eyes, confusion and distress was written all over his features. "I don't know what you've done to me. You've gotten inside my head, fucked with who I am." The pain and anguish in his eyes hit me straight in the chest.

Part of me felt proud—I'd actually gotten through to him. But most of me felt sad. Knowing I affected him just as much as he affected me was harrowing. And I'd never seen him so devastated and needy. It tugged at something deep inside me.

The pull between us was too strong. I wasn't sure how much longer I could hold out. "I just came to make sure you were okay," I choked out.

"I'm fine. Let me drive you home." He rose to his feet.

"You're in no condition to drive." And if there was one thing I couldn't tolerate, it was drunk drivers. Not after the way I'd lost my parents.

"Suit yourself. I'm going to shower then." With the water still running he began undressing, right there in front of me.

I slammed my eyes shut. Oh God. Knox. Naked. My heart banged against my ribs. I should turn around and march out of this bathroom, but my feet were frozen in place.

The shower door opened and Knox cursed as he stepped under what I assumed was scalding hot water. "What are you still doing here, McKenna?" he asked several moments later.

I peeked open one eye, and then the other. Knox stood in the small glass-enclosed shower stall underneath the spray of water, not even bothering to try to cover himself. He was beautiful. All male with sculpted muscles and rugged good looks. He had a dusting of dark hair in all the places a man should, but I forced my eyes up, not wanting to wander any lower than his defined abs and completely visually molest him.

"I-I came to help." *To take care of you.* I swallowed the thick lump in my throat and when I met his dark gaze, something inside me snapped. Without thinking, I pushed open the shower door and was suddenly under that warm spray of water with him. My hands stroked his cheek where it was already swelling, and my fingers pushed into his hair to soothe him. It was my fault he'd gotten hurt and therefore my responsibility to comfort him. Not that being so near him, enveloped in his heat, was any great burden. I felt more alive than ever before under his dark gaze.

"Kenna," he groaned, his eyes falling closed. The tortured cry of my name on his parted lips was the sweetest sound. He stepped closer until our bodies were flush together, brushing at the tops of our thighs, our abdomens, our chests. My heart slammed against my rib cage at the contact. He was pure male heat and my body responded greedily.

168

Desire raced through my veins, heating me from the inside out. I knew this was a bad idea—the worst. Knox was drunk and I was... I didn't know what I was, only that I'd never felt this way before, and I wasn't about to give it up.

We were so close his forehead rested against mine and his lips were just millimeters away from where I wanted them. I'd never wanted anything more than this kiss. We'd been unconsciously building toward this moment since the first time I'd laid eyes on this sinful man. My body knew then what my head could not.

"Kiss me," I whispered.

"And what if I can't stop?" he murmured, his lips brushing against mine.

Pure carnal need like I'd never experienced before shot through me. In that moment, nothing mattered but Knox's hot mouth on mine. "Then don't."

Our mouths were so close that we shared each breath. I breathed him in with each inhalation I drew. The only sounds were my thumping heartbeat crashing in my ears and the spray of water cascading down on us.

His male firmness pressed against my belly and my

breath stuck in my throat. Struggling to breathe, my chest heaved with the effort and brushed against his bare chest. His hands found the hem of my shirt and he lifted the garment up and over my head, slinging the wet fabric to the shower floor where it landed with a smack.

I waited, breathless, to see what he would do. His lips delicately whispered against mine, sending little tingles radiating from my parted lips all the way down to the long-neglected ache in my core. Feelings I'd never known, sensations long dormant, suddenly raged within me, lighting me up from head to toe. I felt awake, fully present for the first time.

I noticed everything, his tender mouth barely brushing mine, the way his dark, hooded eyes roamed from my lips down to the top of my breasts, the way his bare chest glistened in the steam, the tiny water droplets that clung to his eyelashes, and most of all, I noticed my body. I'd never felt more sexual than I did in that moment, standing there in a soaking wet pair of jeans and white bra that was now see-through.

His lips brushed mine a second time and a tiny groan escaped my throat. I'd never imagined he'd be so tender, and the wait was killing me. Knox's mouth came down against me, his warm tongue lightly touching my bottom lip. I opened to accommodate him as my heart rioted in my chest. That little encouragement was all he needed. His mouth pressed hard against mine, his tongue rhythmically stroking, teasing me in the most intimate way. When my tongue matched his, the sensations sent me spiraling out of control.

I lifted up on my toes, wrapping my arms around his strong shoulders, needing something sturdy to ground me. I'd never been kissed like this.

She tasted like sunshine and candy and fucking perfection. I was fighting with myself to go slow, but temptation whispered in my ear, telling me I could have her.

She'd shown up here out of the blue, looking at my bruised cheek like she was the one in pain. It had been a long damn time since I'd been babied, but hell if it didn't feel good. I wanted to feel her soft hands on me, feel her pretty blue eyes caress me like I was someone worthy. But even as my tongue played with hers, my dick rock hard and aching, my fingers itched to touch her, to unclasp her bra and push her jeans down her legs. As the alcohol started to clear from my foggy brain, I knew I needed to slow this down.

I shut off the water and stepped out of the shower, wrapping a towel around my hips and tossing another at McKenna. "Dry off."

Her wide eyes flew to mine, questioning, hurting, but I headed to my room. Dressing quickly in a pair of boxer briefs and jeans, I grabbed a T-shirt and sweatpants for McKenna. They wouldn't fit, but at least she'd have something dry to cover herself with.

That part was critical. My willpower was hanging by a thread.

I tossed the clothes on the end of the bed and turned to see McKenna barefoot and wrapped in a thin white towel across from me. The straps of her wet bra were still peeking over her shoulders.

She dropped her gaze to the floor. "I'm sorry I came."

I crossed the room, fighting the urge to take her in my arms again. "I'm not."

Her face lifted, her eyes full of questions and shimmering with unshed tears. "But you just left me in there…"

"Because I won't take advantage of you."

"You weren't," she whispered, her voice husky.

Christ, she was killing me and she didn't even know it. "I fuck up everything I touch. If you're smart, you'll leave."

She stepped closer. "I must not be very smart then."

Never in my life had I thought so hard about a kiss, but this was McKenna. She wasn't a girl to use once and throw away. She struck a beautiful balance of being both vulnerable and strong.

I knew I shouldn't, that I should dress her and drive her home, but hell, I wanted to taste her sweet lips again. Fuck, I wanted to taste a lot more than that. She was all I'd thought about all night. Cupping her jaw in both hands, I pressed my mouth to hers, trying to be careful, slow, like she needed. But then she was lifting up on her toes and pushing her fingers into my hair, clawing at me to get closer, and I went instantly hard.

When my tongue touched hers again, I stifled a groan. She was like crack cocaine and I wanted more. Wrapping my arms around her to secure her body to mine, the towel around her opened and fell away.

I wanted to admire her gorgeous body, but that would require lifting my mouth from hers and that wasn't an option. I used my hands to explore while my tongue stroked hers. One hand roughly cupping the curve of her ass, and with the other I trailed my fingertips down her thigh.

Her breathing stuttered and I braced my thigh between her legs to support her. She began rubbing herself against me, her damp panties dragging over my thigh again and again.

"Can I touch you?" I asked against her lips.

"Yes," she breathed.

Cupping the generous weight of her breasts in my hands, my thumbs grazed the peaks, which instantly hardened and puckered under my touch. McKenna let out a soft little murmur. The sound sent a jab of lust straight to my balls. My erection was straining against my jeans, barely secured under the waistband, and I took a deep breath, fighting for control.

Still riding my leg, seeking friction between us, McKenna let out a frustrated groan.

She needed more, but I couldn't let us go too far. "Can I touch you over your panties?"

Wide eyes met mine and she nodded slowly. Her look was pure trust and adoration. She was giving me the keys to the kingdom, and I wasn't going to waste this chance. I would make this good for her.

I didn't want to ask her if I could remove them, afraid

she'd say yes, and that I'd take things too far. Besides, the little scrap of fabric wouldn't prevent me from taking care of her. Securing my left arm around her waist to hold her against me, I let my right hand trail down her belly. Little goose bumps erupted over her flesh and her breathing became erratic and much too fast. I loved watching her reactions to even the simplest of touches, although we both knew where my hand was headed, and it wasn't someplace innocent. I wanted to watch her come, to hear her stutter out my name as she gasped for oxygen.

My fingers met the hem of basic white cotton panties and continued lower, past the top of her pubic bone until I felt her warm, damp center. Finding the right spot, I caressed the little nub in circular motions and went back to kissing her, moving my tongue in time with my fingers so I could imagine it was the tip of my tongue swirling against her clit over and over. McKenna's hips bucked against my hand and her head dropped back. I sucked and kissed her throat as incoherent mumbles fell from her lips.

Her fingernails bit into my shoulders, and she sucked in a breath and held it as her body built toward release. Passion burned inside me and I longed to take her to my bed, lay her down and sink inside her warm body. But for once this wasn't about my release, it was all about

McKenna, and watching her come apart was the most erotic sight of my life. She bit her lip, her eyes closed, and her pulse fluttered in her neck. She was beautiful. I continued stroking her most sensitive spot over her panties until I felt her body clenching, preparing for climax.

I held her, kissing her, pleasuring her until she was quivering with her release. She let out a loud gasp and her breath stuttered. Her eyes fell closed and she breathed my name again and again as she came apart in my arms. I held her while little tremors raced through her body, making her shiver.

After several moments she blinked up at me.

"Hi," I offered.

"Hi," she answered, still breathless.

"I set out some dry clothes for you." I tipped my head toward the bed and released her.

She nodded and crossed the room to grab them off the bed, then headed into the bathroom to change. Even after what we'd just done, she wasn't going to change in front of me. She was surprisingly modest for someone who'd just gotten off riding my hand.

I killed the lights, then crawled under the covers and waited.

Soon McKenna was wandering toward me in the dark. Even the lack of light couldn't hide the healthy glow I'd put in her cheeks.

She lay down beside me, curling into a ball so that we lay facing each other. We were both quiet, likely both processing what had happened between us tonight. We just lay there watching each other in the dim light.

I had no idea how many laws or rules I'd broken getting it on with my sex addiction counselor, and I didn't want to know. I'd done a whole lot of sexy shit over the years, but I'd never had anything get me as hot as what I just did with McKenna.

The anticipation of it, knowing how hard I've had to work to win her over these past several weeks, getting her to trust me and let go. It felt huge, and I was happy. Leaving her panties in place like that and watching her writhe against my fingers, knowing she was soaking wet and ready for me, it made me wonder how good she tasted, how pink she would be, and it had made me so hard.

And the craziest thing was, I didn't want to rush her.

I mean, yeah, I wanted to pull her panties down her legs, but in a way, I didn't. I liked that next time there would be more for us to discover.

I was going slow with a girl. And I liked it.

The shower and our little post-shower activities had seemed to sober Knox up. He lay there quietly watching me, his eyes clear and focused.

"Thank you for letting me stay over tonight," I said. I assumed this was a big deal for him—a girl in his bed who wasn't here for sex.

"It's not a problem," he whispered.

"I'm sorry about what happened tonight with Brian."

"You have nothing to be sorry for. I really don't like the idea of your living with that guy, though."

"He'd never do anything to hurt me."

"How did you end up living with him?"

I took a deep breath. Knox didn't know the story, and since I knew so much about him, I was starting to feel guilty for never telling him. "I lost my parents my senior year of high school." I wasn't ready to explain how it had happened or my role in the events, so I didn't. "My mom was an only child and my dad's only brother, my uncle

180

Bob, had passed away two years before of a stroke. My aunt Linda, who I'm only related to because she was married to my uncle, lives in California and I didn't want to change schools, so I moved in with Brian's parents to finish my senior year of school."

"I'm sorry about your parents."

"Thank you," I murmured. I didn't want to dampen the evening by thinking about all that, so instead I pushed on. "And when I moved here after college, Brian came with me. He didn't want me to live in a new city all alone."

"Nice guy," Knox muttered flatly.

I swatted at his chest. "Thank you for…tonight." God, what had I been about to say, thank you for that orgasm? I'd never had an orgasm like that before. My cheeks heated.

Knox chuckled. "You can have that anytime you want. No need to thank me."

I chewed on my lip, working up my courage. "Isn't that hard for you, though? I mean, doing that with me, having me here and knowing it's not going to go any further?"

He was quiet for a second while he thought about it.

"Yes and no. Trust me, I enjoyed it, and as far as it not going any further…I can manage."

"I like you so open and vulnerable like this," I whispered.

"Yeah? Well, enjoy it now then. I'm never like this."

"I know."

"Do you?"

"Yes, you're normally so intense, and dominant."

"Do you even understand what that word means, McKenna?"

"I think so." A crease lined my forehead. Maybe I didn't really know. At least, not in the context of how he thought of himself.

"I am dominant. Sexually. Does that scare you?"

"N-no?"

He chuckled lightly. I hadn't meant my answer to sound like a question. It only showed how unsure I felt around him.

"Good night, McKenna."

"'Night, Knox," I murmured, feeling sleepy and

warm. And safe.

Chapter Fourteen

When I arrived home the following morning, I thought it best that Knox not walk me inside. I said good-bye to him in the car and ventured in to face Brian alone.

Just as I suspected, Brian was waiting for me. Probably waiting to ambush me. He flipped off the TV and rose from the couch, coming to meet me near the door.

"Did you stay the night with him?"

"Brian," I pleaded. My tone was a warning. He didn't get to act the way he did last night and then give me the third degree this morning. Besides, I didn't want to crush him or make him angry by confirming what he already knew. I'd slept in Knox's bed last night and it was one of the best night's sleep I'd had in years. I figured it was safer not to answer, so instead I released a heavy sigh.

"Tell me you're not stupid enough to fall for this guy. He's a goddamn sex addict, McKenna."

"Don't call me stupid." I pushed past him and entered the kitchen, grabbing the coffeepot and filling it with water.

"I'm sorry, I know you're not...it's just..." He rubbed the back of his neck, looking down at the scuffed tile floor. He looked tired, like he'd barely slept last night, and his face was pinched with worry.

It made my stomach cramp seeing him so distraught. Brian had always been there for me and he'd been a great friend for almost fifteen years. He'd messed up last night, but without him, I wouldn't have survived these past few years. I just didn't know why he was acting so ridiculous about Knox.

"I get it," he said. "You're a fixer, you always have been, and he's a project, but he's not like that cocker spaniel you found on the side of the road with a broken leg. You can't fix everything, and you sure as hell can't play house with him."

"Too late for that, isn't it, Bri?" I shoved the carafe back into the coffee machine and set it to brew. When I looked up at him, really looked at him, I noticed his lip was split and there was a bruise forming under his eye. Served him right for attacking Knox like he did.

Brian sighed. "I'm sorry I flipped out last night. I just don't want to lose you."

The sight of him and Knox fighting on our living room floor was burned into my retinas. I was glad neither was seriously hurt. Knox's cheek was still slightly swollen this morning, but nothing that a little ice and pain reliever wouldn't fix.

I tried to look at things from Brian's perspective. We'd moved here together and neither of us knew a soul, and now I was forming a relationship with another man. My anger faded just slightly. "I won't condone any more testosterone-fueled displays like last night. You're my best friend. Knox is my…" I stuttered, coming to a halt midsentence. What was Knox?

"He's your what, McKenna?" Brian challenged.

"Friend," I settled on finally. "So you have to be nice."

Stuffing his hands in his pockets, Brian nodded. "For you, I'll try. But just be careful with that guy."

"I will," I promised. I would be careful with him, I just hoped he would be careful with me too. I was terrified of feeling something real for him, unsure if he was capable of returning those feelings.

Chapter Fifteen

The rest of the week passed quickly. Brian seemed to chill out a little, not mentioning Knox again and being overly helpful at home. He was trying to make up for how he had acted, though I wondered if his change in mood was because I hadn't seen Knox again.

Things had gotten busy at the center for troubled teens, and even though I only worked there part-time during the week, I found myself going in early and staying late. They were short staffed, so I'd added extra hours to my schedule without having to be asked. And since I still had my weekly commitments at the homeless shelter, soup kitchen, and others, I was exhausted at the end of the day.

Knox and I had texted a few times, and I wondered if both of us were subconsciously trying to slow things down between us after how heated they'd gotten the last time I saw him.

After sleeping in later than planned, I was running late for my Saturday morning meeting. The only thing that kept me from being really late was the bus had cooperated and been on time. When I entered the room, I found the members of our group already seated in a semicircle. Someone had even brewed the coffee. I breathed a sigh of relief. Everything was in order.

Crossing the room to the front, my eyes strayed to Knox. He'd turned to face the girl next to him—someone I'd never seen before. She appeared to be about our age, petite and very pretty with shiny coppery hair and big green eyes. Suddenly I realized that this must be Amanda.

Belinda was right. Despite being a few months pregnant, she wasn't showing at all. In fact, she had on a pair of skintight leggings that showed off how slender she was, and an off-the-shoulder white tee.

Tearing my eyes away from her, I realized Knox was still chatting with the girl and hadn't even noticed me. I slid into my seat and cleared my throat. Amanda and Knox ended their conversation, and I kicked off our session. But the little impish smile remained fixed on Amanda's lips long after her chat with Knox.

Somehow, seeing firsthand the effect he had on women bothered me even more than it should have. I wanted to separate their chairs, position myself between them, but of course I didn't. I just continued right on with group, trying to remain professional.

"Amanda, right?" I looked at the new girl and she nodded her head. "Welcome. I'm glad you're here." My voice sounded genuine, but if she was going to move in on Knox, that would change in a heartbeat. I would be the only one tempting him, thank you very much. "Why don't you introduce yourself and tell us whatever you're comfortable starting with."

"Sure. Hi, everyone. I'm Amanda." She looked around at the faces in the group and smiled. She went on to explain that she grew up in the foster care system, and no one had wanted her—or at least that was how she felt, and so she sought man after man to supplement those feelings. She used sex to cope—to feel wanted—if only for a short time. Then of course when it was over, she felt worse than ever.

It was a tragic cycle I'd heard before, and I honestly hoped I could help her break it. This work was hard, but I never gave up hope of actually getting through to someone. It made it all worthwhile. Amanda didn't mention her pregnancy, so I assumed she wanted to keep that to herself.

I moved on, asking what other updates people wanted to share. As Mia spoke about her recent breakthrough, I knew I should feel happy and proud. Instead I was struck with a sense of worry. The closer I got to Knox, the more I'd worry about his past with women, and if it was truly all in his past. The realization was harrowing. Would we ever really be able to move forward from the demons that haunted us?

The possibility that his sexual addiction could come between us terrified me. Would I be used and then tossed aside like so many before me? I was smarter than that, wasn't I? Brian's concerns had obviously gotten inside my head.

"McKenna?" Mia asked, her brows drawn together in question.

Twelve sets of eyes were peering right at me. How long had I been lost in my own thoughts? A quick glance at the clock told me far too long. Our hour was up, and a few people were already zipping up coats and jingling car keys in their hands. *Oops.*

"Thank you, everyone. See you next time."

Amanda turned right back to Knox, like she'd spent the entire hour just itching to strike up their conversation again.

Wiping the scowl from my face, I rose from my seat and went to the desk at the front of the room. As curious as I was about what they could be discussing, I forced myself to focus on something else. I wanted to talk to Knox, to tell him I hadn't stopped thinking about that night, but the more time that passed, the more foolish I felt.

Several minutes later, Amanda rose to her feet and slung her purse over her shoulder. She fished her cell phone from the bag and it appeared that she and Knox were exchanging phone numbers. A searing pain stabbed at my chest.

I shouldn't have been so hungry for his touch. It hadn't been my smartest moment. But I wasn't a normal girl. I was damaged emotionally and had felt so alone for the last few years that I craved physical touch. From a sex addict. A man like Knox wouldn't savor those simple touches like I did. He wouldn't be lying in bed tonight thinking about how his hand had felt brushing over my skin like I would be. He used women, took his pleasure and moved on.

Maybe it was time I did the same thing. I grabbed my

purse from the desk and fled.

I dressed and ventured downstairs. Tucker was sitting cross-legged on the living room floor, watching a cartoon I knew he'd seen three hundred times. But his science project was done, so I wouldn't complain.

Jaxon and Luke were stationed together at the dining room table, and Luke was helping him with algebra. "Dude, what the fuck did you eat?" Jaxon asked, pushing Luke's shoulder to gain some distance between them.

"I don't know. I had Chinese earlier. Why?" Luke responded, sniffing his breath through a cupped palm.

"It smells like garlic and farts. It's fucking burning my nostrils, dude. Go get some gum or something. I can't concentrate on math when my eyes are watering."

Luke stuffed three sticks of gum into his mouth. "Happy?"

"Very," Jaxon said dryly.

"Guys, you're on your own tonight. I'll be at Gus's Pub till probably two. Call and order pizza." I handed

Luke a twenty-dollar bill. "Lock the doors, and stay in. Got it?" They nodded in unison. "And call me if you need me."

I wondered if McKenna would still be stopping over, and what she'd think when the guys told her I wasn't here. I pushed the thoughts from my head. It wasn't my problem. We both probably needed to move on before things got even more complicated. I crossed the room and ruffled Tucker's hair to say good-bye. Then buttoned up my black dress shirt and headed out into the night.

Gus's was an Irish tavern that I tended bar at occasionally. Thursday nights were usually good for at least two hundred bucks in tips, and so when Rachel had called earlier and said they were short staffed, I'd jumped at the opportunity. We could use the cash, and I knew if I stayed in tonight, I'd end up calling McKenna.

"Hey, hot stuff." Rachel smacked my ass in greeting.

"What's up?" I nodded her way. She bent over at the waist, stocking the cooler with bottles of beer. Rachel was gorgeous and she knew it. She was tall and slender with long bleached-blonde hair and cherry-red lips. A series of girly tattoos made up a half sleeve on her right arm—butterflies, flowers, hearts, things like that. I was convinced a lot of our male patrons came in just to hit on Rachel.

"Sammy's out tonight and so is one of our bar backs, so we'll be busy. Hope you can handle it."

"I think you know I can." I'd been working here on and off for four years. I knew the place inside and out. Just because I didn't maintain regular shifts didn't mean shit. Tending bar was like riding a bike. Put a shaker and a bottle in my hand, and I knew what to do.

"Cocky much?" she teased, winking at me beneath thick black lashes.

"It's not cocky if it's true." I jumped into action, punching in at the register and grabbing a crate of glasses to stack beneath the bar.

The evening crowd began to filter in and take up seats at the bar and the nearby high-top tables. Rachel and I managed to keep up our easy banter while mixing drinks and pouring beers from the tap. She flicked a beer cap at my chest. "Hey, lover boy." She nodded her head toward the far end of the bar. "Looks like you have a visitor."

My eyes followed Rachel's stare to the end of the bar, where I spotted her. McKenna. Guilt burned in my subconscious for my actions the other night. I couldn't believe how far I'd let things go.

"Cover me for a second?" I called out to Rachel, already making my way toward the end of the bar.

McKenna looked completely out of place here. Her gaze darted around at the jostling bodies as her hands clutched at the shoulder strap of her purse, holding it securely around her body. When her eyes met mine, her expression softened just slightly. She stepped closer to the bar, sliding onto an open stool in front of her. The guy immediately to her left smiled and pushed himself closer.

When I approached, McKenna's eyes lifted to mine and she bit her lip, seemingly unsure about being here. Damn right, she should feel unsure. This place was a meat market and she was a delicious, juicy steak.

The douche bag next to her lifted his hand to get my attention. "Another beer and whatever this pretty young thing wants."

McKenna's eyes widened, as if she suddenly realized that coming alone to a bar might not have been the best call. But I wouldn't let anything happen to her.

I leaned closer, getting in the guy's face. "You're done here. I'm not serving you anything more, and you sure as shit aren't buying her a drink. I suggest you leave."

"What the—"

I slammed a fist onto the bar and the guy quickly rose and took off.

"Why'd you do that?" she asked, looking bewildered.

I wouldn't explain my actions to her. Not until she explained some things to me first. "Why did you come here?"

"Your brothers said you were out. I was worried you were—"

"Out drinking and picking up women?" I supplied.

She nodded.

"Nope. Just working." Christ, she was watching me with those pretty sapphire-blue eyes, looking at me like she was both hurt and disappointed. I turned to the guy next to us. "What can I get for you?"

"Bud Light," he called back. I cracked open a bottle and handed it to him, punching the order into the register to add it to his tab before turning back to McKenna.

"No freebies, honey. You want something to drink?" Rachel said to McKenna, suddenly standing next to me.

"She's a friend, Rachel. Back off."

Rachel laughed, throwing her head back. "Yeah, they're all your friends until morning. Right, Knox?"

Curiosity burned in McKenna's gaze as she appraised Rachel. Looking back and forth between us, I could see the wheels in McKenna's head spinning, wondering about my history with this feisty blonde. All it took was one little look from McKenna and I felt unworthy of her. This would never work. Why was she here? Didn't she get the memo after the other night? Unless she was back for more...

McKenna pulled her gaze from Rachel to focus back on me, and straightened her shoulders. "What time do you get off?"

"Two," I croaked, wondering what she was doing.

"I'll wait then. Give me a Diet Coke, please."

Rachel rolled her eyes and stormed away. Shit, I didn't know what her problem was with McKenna being here. As long as I did my job, she shouldn't care that McKenna was hanging out at the end of the bar.

"What are you planning to do? Stay here and babysit me, make sure I go straight home after my shift?" She didn't respond. In any other circumstance it might have angered me, but coming from McKenna, I knew her concern was genuine. "If we have any chance, you have to trust me, angel."

Her eyes flashed on mine. "Do you trust yourself?"

I leaned closer. "Around you? No."

Blush colored her cheeks. "I went to your house. I still owe you guys dinner, and when Luke told me you were here—at a bar—what was I supposed to think?"

"The worst, apparently."

Her gaze zeroed in on Rachel, who was still watching us with a scowl. "Have you slept with that girl?" She tipped her head toward the end of the bar where Rachel was polishing pint glasses.

Shit. "Once. A long time ago."

Her face fell.

"Hey…" I reached for her hand and brought it to my lips. "I'd be happy if you stayed tonight and waited for me."

She chewed on her lip, as if deciding.

The truth was, I trusted myself completely around Rachel. We'd had sex once, two years ago, shortly after she began working here. And despite her constant flirting with me, I saw it strictly as a one-time thing. If McKenna was willing to hang out here all night, I wouldn't deny myself the chance to be near her.

"Do you want me to order you some food? We have a full kitchen."

"Sure. What's good here?" She leaned toward me, settling in.

Just after one in the morning, Rachel told me to go ahead and punch out. The crowd had died down, but mostly I think she'd grown tired of watching me and McKenna steal glances at each other all night. Normally I'd feel bad leaving a coworker with all the end-of-shift cleaning, but I was itching to be alone with McKenna again.

I punched out in back and washed up before meeting McKenna. She slid off her stool and stretched. "Now what?"

I wanted to get her alone in my bedroom again, but I knew I needed to reel myself in before I pushed her too far. "Whatever you like."

"Can we just go back to your place?"

"The guys will be sleeping." I needed her to understand what she was asking me for. We'd be alone with nothing to distract me and no one to protect her.

She lifted up on her toes and leaned in until her lips brushed my ear. "I'll be quiet."

Blood raged south to my groin, making me instantly hard. "Come on."

Chapter Sixteen

With my heart slamming into my ribs, I climbed the stairs to Knox's room, thinking about the first time I'd come here. Just like I could feel his gaze on me then, I could feel it now. Only this time, I knew what his hands felt like on my skin, what his hot mouth felt like moving against mine.

When I reached his bedroom, I wanted to be brave, to show him what I wanted, since I knew I wouldn't have the guts to tell him how I felt. Instead, I stopped awkwardly in the center of the room and stared at the big bed.

From behind me, Knox's warm hand came to rest on my shoulder. The heat from his body licked mine, warming me from head to toe. "Relax," he breathed behind my ear.

As if on command, my body instantly relaxed. This was Knox. He might have his issues, but he'd never hurt me. I opened my mouth to tell him I was fine, but let out a huge yawn instead. *Oops*. It seemed my body suddenly remembered the late hour.

"You're tired." Knox chuckled, coming around to face me.

I nodded. "I'm sleepy."

"Go lay down on my bed. I'm going to take a quick shower."

I obeyed, toeing off my shoes and padding across the room in my socks to crawl into his big bed. I pulled the covers around me and snuggled against his pillow. *Mmm.* That scent I'd come to love—sandalwood, leather, and male deliciousness—greeted me.

Sometime later, Knox crawled into bed beside me and I opened my eyes to watch him in the pale moonlight position himself on the pillow. He met my gaze and grinned. "Did I wake you?"

I nodded. "I dozed off waiting for you."

"It's okay. You can rest, sleepy girl. You're safe."

I did feel safe with him. Even the other night, things had only gone as far as I'd wanted them to. In fact, Knox had been somewhat reluctant, leaving me in the shower alone and dressing in the other room. Not that I'd had to convince him too much. His body had responded to the intensity between us just like mine had. His erection had been impossible not to notice. I hadn't been brave enough to touch him, even though I'd wanted to. In fact, it was all I'd thought about while lying in bed this week.

Knox was still watching me. He hadn't yet touched me, but he didn't have to. I could feel the heat from his body as his hot breath warmed a path across my skin. I nestled myself closer and he opened his arms for me, embracing me securely against his body.

"Knox?"

"Hmm?"

Losing my courage, I shrugged. "I'm not tired anymore." I wanted to ask him about his recovery, if he'd been abstaining from sex, but I knew I wasn't brave enough to hear the answer.

"What do you want?" He groaned, breathless.

Part of me couldn't believe I'd found myself in his bed again, tempting him. I shouldn't be here, even if it was exactly where I wanted to be. I didn't even know where he stood with his recovery. He kept that information closely guarded.

"Never mind. Maybe we should just sleep," I said, even though it was the last thing I wanted.

"You see, there's this girl who's making it a little *hard* at the moment."

When he emphasized the word *hard,* I giggled. "Knox?" I asked again.

"Yeah?"

I took a deep breath, drawing my courage. "How have you been doing with your addiction?"

He paused for several seconds, a long, awkward silence hanging between us. "I've cut back."

My stomach tightened into a knot. "Why don't you just stop?"

"Where's the fun in that?" he teased, poking me in the ribs underneath the covers.

"Recovering from an addiction isn't supposed to be fun." I arranged the blankets around me, feeling the sudden need to create a barrier between us.

"Who says I have an addiction? Maybe I just hang out with you on Saturday mornings because I want to."

"Your counselor, that's me, says you do, and I bet

your brothers too if we asked them."

"McKenna…"

His tone held a warning, but I pressed on. "What, Knox?"

"I do what I need to do. Are you offering up your services?"

My breathing pattern changed. It was like my body forgot the simple process of drawing in air and releasing it back out. "I'm serious. I'm here, Knox. I believe in you, but…"

I swallowed down a lump in my throat. I couldn't take it to know he was still the same man he was before we met. I'd shared pieces of myself with him, made myself completely vulnerable, and I needed to know he was meeting me halfway.

"Listen, I'm not saying I'm a hundred percent, or that I'll never slip up, but I have been trying, McKenna."

My heart crashed violently against my ribs. It wasn't a promise, it wasn't any sort of guarantee, but nothing with him ever would be. I had to decide if I could accept that. My head said no, but my lonely heart was willing to try. I rolled closer, needing to feel the shelter his warm body provided.

Knox was trying. It might not be much, but knowing I'd inspired change in him meant everything. It meant maybe I was doing something right, that my hard work was beginning to pay off. As I lay there with him, warm and secure, I never wanted this moment to end. The vulnerability he showed me, his belief that things would turn out okay, it was all so fragile, but it was all I had.

Wrapping his arm around my middle to snuggle me in closer, his big palm came to a rest on my exposed hip, sending a tiny thrill zipping through me. My entire body buzzed with awareness. I wanted to pretend he was mine, that this was all normal—me and him alone in his bed. I wanted to touch him. We were so close, I could feel the heat from his skin and smell his scent—a combination of body wash and a slight hint of mint toothpaste. The urge to nuzzle into his neck and feel the stubble from his jaw scrape my skin rose up inside me. Instead I remained rooted in place, my breathing growing shallow and rapid as desire for him raced through my system.

I would never be able to sleep in this state. My heart slammed against my ribs, nearly knocking the breath from my lungs. "There's something I want to try."

"What's that?" he asked, his voice strained.

"Do you think I could…touch you?"

He swallowed heavily, his Adam's apple moving in the dim light. "You want to touch me?"

I knew this was hard for him—being physical without having sex—but maybe it was good for him too. Like stretching before a workout, he had to develop these muscles if he wanted to grow stronger, if he wanted to heal.

"Would that be bad?" I bit my lip, sort of liking the idea of being naughty after being good for so long. I wanted to feel his warmth, to make sure what I felt blooming inside me was real. That he was real.

"I'm pretty sure that would be really bad. One touch from you and I'd probably embarrass myself."

I pouted, though I was almost positive he couldn't see my expression. "What do you mean?"

He drew a breath and released it slowly through clenched teeth. "You have no idea how badly I want you. You're beautiful, smart, talented, kind, and good to your very core. Touching me will only taint you, as bad as I might want it."

He wouldn't decide this for me. Knox was a good man, despite his history. I placed my palm flat on his bare abs and felt him tense. "Will you show me?"

"Show you?"

"What you like," I said, recovering. I didn't want him to know how inexperienced I really was.

"Fuck," he bit out. "McKenna, we shouldn't do this."

My hand curled into a fist, retracting away from him. "Do you not want to?"

He cursed again. "Trust me, that's not it. You get my dick so hard, but it's more than that. *You're* more than that."

My heart soared. Hearing him acknowledge that I was something special to him did strange things to me. And the fact that I turned him on despite my lack of knowledge...it made my heart pound like a drum and my panties grow damp.

Uncurling my fingers, I flattened my palm against his stomach and again felt his jerky inhale. I let my hand begin to trail south. A dusting of fine hairs tickled my palm as I lightly caressed him. When I reached the waistband of his boxer briefs, Knox sucked in a breath and held it. Not yet brave enough to feel him skin to skin, I brushed my hand against his erection and warmth flooded my panties.

I rubbed the length of his manhood as my heart thundered in my chest. My confidence growing, I rubbed him up and down, feeling bold and powerful. He felt thick and long, and I wanted to see him.

"Kenna…" He groaned, sending a little rush of tingles skittering out over my skin.

As my endorphins kicked in, my inexperience no longer mattered. I felt alive, and I wanted this—to touch this beautiful, broken man, to be part of making him whole again.

My fingers edged into the waistband of his boxers and Knox lifted his hips slightly off the mattress, allowing me to pull them down and free his heavy cock.

Under the faintest glow of moonlight, I admired his body—his strength, masculinity, and the tender way he was watching me. He was making himself vulnerable to me, letting me take control and do things at my own pace. The emotional weight of the moment left me breathless. But then my gaze lowered and my breath caught in my throat. He was huge.

Curling my hand around him, I was surprised to feel how soft and smooth the skin was despite being rock hard and turgid beneath my grasp. As I ran my fingertips up and down the length of him, Knox let out a breathy groan. My core clenched. The idea of him filling me left me warm and achy. My palm slid lightly against him, gently massaging and caressing his considerable length as I savored the feel of him. Lightly rubbing smooth, hot flesh, I watched in fascination as he grew even harder.

Knox wrapped his hand over mine, increasing the pressure of my grip. "Like this." Our hands moving together, he dictated the pace of our movements until I was rhythmically stroking him from base to tip.

He released a shuddering breath and his head fell back against the pillow. "Fuck, your hand feels good."

My pace increased as I watched Knox's reactions. His warm breath puffed past his lips, his abs tensed, and his hand found my free one, intertwining our fingers. He pressed his palm to mine like he was sinking and I had the power to pull him back to safety. He gripped my hand and his dark gaze met mine. He communicated so much with that one look.

Emotion burned inside me. I was discovering him,

but this moment meant more than that. We were healing each other in these little moments built on shared trust.

"Shit, I'm going to—" His teeth bit into his lower lip as his body went rigid. He growled my name as he came, milky-white fluid landing on his belly.

While our breathing slowed, Knox reached over the side of the bed for a box of tissues on the floor. He wiped my hand and his belly before curling his arms around me, caging me in. I melted into his embrace, loving the feel of his strong arms. He could hold me hostage in his bed anytime.

"Sorry about the mess," he apologized, whispering near my ear.

"I didn't mind." Watching Knox come apart and hearing his low husky voice growl my name had been worth it.

Meeting my eyes with an intense, passion-filled stare, he leaned closer, resting his forehead against mine. "You didn't have to do that."

I knew that. I'd wanted to. "Was it…okay?"

"That was fucking amazing." He pressed his lips softly to mine in a lingering kiss. "I like you in my bed," he whispered.

His admission meant the world to me. I kissed him back, my movements slow and deliberate, like every touch mattered.

During quiet times like this, I loved how open and exposed he made himself to me. I knew it was a side of himself he didn't share with anyone else, and that feeling was addicting.

Chapter Seventeen

Last night had been the most incredible experience of my life. I had slept soundly in Knox's arms all through the night. I smiled remembering our whispered conversation, and the way my heartbeat had thrummed so violently in my chest when I'd touched him. He was beautiful, and he wasn't broken like he thought.

Then this morning was back to reality. We'd kissed good-bye early this morning. I wanted to go home to shower and change, and most importantly to arrive at our meeting separately. Even if I was breaking all the rules with Knox behind closed doors, I certainly wouldn't broadcast it in public.

I sat at my little wooden desk at the front of the room, having arrived several minutes early, unable to stop myself from daydreaming about him. The more time I spent with Knox, the less I noticed that hollow ache inside me. I sang in the shower, hummed when I cleaned the dishes, and felt lighter just knowing he was in my life.

But then I realized something even more terrifying than going back to my pre-Knox state. I was falling in love with him. With a deliciously flawed man I was supposed to be helping heal from sexual addiction.

Casting logic aside, I knew this was a dangerous game, and if I played I'd likely be burned. But falling for him hadn't been a choice. He wasn't just that haunted, intense man I'd glimpsed at first. He was different around his brothers, lighter, laughed easier, smiled that big smile that showed off his dimple. I liked that version of Knox. And I liked the version of myself when I was with him. I wasn't the broken shell of a girl I felt like most days. I felt vibrant and pretty and alive.

I wondered if my attraction to him was that our souls shared the same pain and loss. They could feel each other. When we were together I didn't feel any pain or guilt. I wondered if it was the same for him.

When he entered the room, my heart's rhythm changed, became erratic. His eyes met mine and while his face remained expressionless, I read the indecision, the confusion on him as clear as day. Did he feel guilty about what happened between us last night? It had been my idea to touch him, to push things further, and as much as I'd enjoyed it at the time, now I felt unsure and guilty.

Amanda patted the seat next to her, one that she'd clearly been saving just for him, and Knox crossed the room toward her.

Watching him and Amanda converse quietly, my stomach tightened and I felt hot. I was warm and flustered, and now I needed to start group.

I sat down in my seat and began the lecture I'd prepared. "Today we'll be working on openness and honesty with each other. We've been meeting for several weeks now, and it's time we progressed as a group. I'm going to ask each member of the group to share their progress, and this includes admitting to any slipups in a judgment-free, guilt-free environment. We're all human, and it's here that we don't have to hide."

I consulted the notebook on my lap to be sure I'd touched on all the key points I'd written out for myself. Knox watched me closely, his expression guarded and unsure. Guilt clawed at my stomach. I'd orchestrated today's entire conversation to flush out what he was too afraid to tell me. I needed to know.

I asked each member of the group to share how many days since their last sexual encounter. As each person

217

spoke and Knox's turn got closer, my stomach coiled tight and nervous energy shot through my veins. Something was about to happen.

It was Amanda's turn next, so I forced my eyes from Knox, trying to be a good group leader and listen as she spoke. "I've been struggling with a lot of change in my life lately, and I'm not proud of it, but I slipped up last weekend. It's been one week of celibacy now for me."

I nodded and gave her a tender smile, and then my eyes swung back over to Knox.

"Same here. One week," he choked out.

Several things struck me at once and my brain fought to catch up. He wasn't counting our time together last night, probably because it hadn't led to sex, and his length of abstinence matched Amanda's perfectly. They'd exchanged phone numbers one week ago at the end of group and...what? Met up for sex that day? My body broke out in a cold sweat and my heartbeat rang in my ears.

With my windpipe threatening to close and tears shimmering in my eyes, I jumped from my seat and fled the room. I ran blindly down the hall, tears burning my vision and a rock-solid lump in my chest. It would have been one thing for him to drunkenly mess up with a stranger before we started really seeing each other, but planning a sex date with a member of our group?

I heard my name being called behind me and pushed my legs faster. I couldn't have anyone see me break down like this. I felt betrayed and humiliated. Why had I ever thought I could do this? Change this man and have something meaningful. I was an idiot. I'd been living in the fantasy of it. Being near Knox had made me feel better about my own life, but all of that had just come crashing to a close.

"McKenna! Stop!" Knox called behind me, closer this time.

I gripped the door handle to the stairwell, threw it open, and ran down two flights of stairs before I collapsed in a heap. I couldn't breathe, could only feel my heart clenching and dying inside my chest. I huddled against the wall, sobbing uncontrollably while tears and snot streaked my face.

Knox sank to his knees in front of me. "McKenna?"

I wiped my cheeks with the back of my hand and drew a short, shuddering breath. "When were you last with someone, Knox?"

"Other than you?" he asked, his brows pinched together as though he was the one angry about something.

I nodded.

He released a deep sigh and looked down. A thick, uncomfortable silence settled between us. My heart slammed against my ribs and with each second of his silence, my doubts only grew.

"She's pregnant, you know."

His eyes snapped up to mine. "Who?"

"Amanda," I croaked.

He didn't respond at first. He just sat there, silently blinking at me. "I know."

If he was still doing what he used to, I couldn't let it go. I couldn't move past it. Selfishly, I needed all of him. I needed him to be stronger because I most certainly was not strong enough for this. He was breaking me apart and I didn't even think he knew it.

"I thought I could do this. I thought I was strong enough, but I'm not. Not at all." A hiccup escaped my throat as I realized everything I'd be losing. Instead of constantly beating myself up, I'd focused on fixing Knox. And now I had no idea what good that had done me or where we stood.

"I can't stand by and watch you use random girls and then cuddle with me at night like everything is fine."

Angry hands tore through his hair, leaving it standing in disarray. Our happy memories of just last night seemed like so long ago. "You think this is a surprise for me? I told you I'd fuck this up."

I hated hearing him admitting defeat, for not fighting for this—for me. When he was ready to change and grow, he would. I'd wanted to be part of his growth process, but it seemed I hadn't been. I wasn't the girl to change him.

"I'm not right for you. I'm all hard edges and a mistake-riddled past. I'm too fucked up for someone like you. You have to see that. No amount of counseling or talking will fix the shit I've done, McKenna. You should leave while you can."

I was quiet while he spoke, my head empty and my heart in tatters. Knox was trouble; I should say good-bye and move on with my life. I needed to stop playing house with him and his brothers before it was too late.

I just didn't want to.

Stay Tuned for...

When I Surrender

Coming soon!

Undaunted by Knox's complicated history with sexual addiction, McKenna pushes forward in her relationship with this deliciously flawed man. She experiences the highest highs as they discover each other, along with the lowest lows, and worries that his past may not be entirely behind him.

But when a complication from her own past demands attention, she is forced to decide where their relationship is headed, and everything she thought she knew is questioned.

When I Surrender is Book 2 in the WHEN I BREAK series.

Warning:

Contains explicit content, recommended for readers 17+.

Acknowledgments

Thank you to all my fabulously wonderful readers who continue to read the books I release and support me in the indie community. You are a blessing. Thank you to my beta readers Holly, Heather, and Sarah. I truly appreciate your feedback.

I am bowing down on my knees to thank the amazingly talented Pam Berehulke from Bulletproof Editing for your magic with this manuscript. I am thrilled that Jenn Sterling made the introductions for us, and you were able to squeeze me in.

To my family, whose love and support makes this all possible. I love you.

Other Titles by Kendall Ryan

Unravel Me

Make Me Yours

Resisting Her

Hard to Love

The Impact of You

Working It

Craving Him

All or Nothing

Visit Kendall Ryan at:

www.kendallryanbooks.com

www.facebook.com/kendallryanbooks

www.twitter.com/kendallryan1